THEORY OF REALITY

THEORY OF REALITY

PART 1

ELI MENDOZA

NEW DEGREE PRESS

COPYRIGHT © 2021 ELI MENDOZA

THEORY OF REALITY

Part 1

ISBN   978-1-63676-925-7   *Paperback*

            978-1-63676-989-9   *Kindle Ebook*

            978-1-63730-093-0   *Ebook*

CONTENTS

NOTE FROM THE AUTHOR

———

As an avid reader in childhood, I related to all types of unique characters in the many books I read. *But none were quite like me.*

The teen novels available to me focused on one trait of one character. They were smart, mentally ill, bullied, had mixed identities, had family issues, had a secret, *or* were LGBTQ+, but never all together. I want to be more intersectional about things. Why? Because intersectionality exists. I am of mixed ethnicity, am part of the LGBTQ+ community, and deal with mental and chronic illness. Identity consists of various pieces, and these pieces combine to create varying experiences—which is what intersectionality means. Coined by Kimberlé Crenshaw in 1989, the concept of intersectionality has become increasingly important as society works toward embracing diversity and equity.[1]

———

1   *Merriam-Webster*, s.v. "intersectionality (*n.*)," accessed March 15, 2021.

It's hard enough to be a teenager dealing with bad situations or even just being "the new kid." It's even more complicated if you happen to be different from those around you in terms of race, ethnicity, sexuality, gender, mental health, neurotype, or disability. My book shows that even in diverse areas such as Rosedale, complex identities can be a source of beauty and at the same time pose significant problems. Trauma does not discriminate.

After reading James Patterson's *Witch and Wizard* series, I became obsessed with the idea of multiple perspectives, because it allows an author to explore such questions as:

- How do different people react differently, or similarly, to one another?
- How can someone's perceptions of situations change depending on their backgrounds and identities?
- How do the small actions of other people impact our own environments?

By providing characters with complex identities, I hope to prompt discussions about mental illness and help reduce stigma. Adults should no longer tell teens that their feelings or identity are "just hormones." Undiagnosed mental issues, medical neglect, relying on friends (or worse, your own mind), and navigating new situations on your own can be overwhelming and dangerous. I will always recommend teens talking to a trusted adult about issues if they feel safe doing so, but that is not always an option. So, for those who feel they have no safe resource, I offer this book as an escape; as a way to alleviate the strong impostor syndrome we face by seeing a world where their identity exists and is validated. I hope everyone who picks up this book finds a way to understand the characters and relate, even in a small way, to their struggles. Part of intersectional identity is understanding we are not really all that different from each other. I hope that with this book, I'm able to bring in representation that celebrates the diversity in every individual.

1

EMILY

Monday. First day of tenth grade. Time to see everyone in Rosedale I have not seen in eleven weeks. I wear my usual outfit: a T-shirt, jeans, a black hooded jacket, fingerless gloves, and classic Chuck Taylors. Even my shoulder-length brown hair is the same. My mom never lets me cut it above my ear-lobes. She's had those weirdly specific rules since I came out to her as transgender just before starting high school. Ever since then, my identity has stagnated. I thought I could be a new me in 2010 to start off the decade, but it's been years since then. It feels like all the 2010s will be the same.

I place myself in the second row from the back of the old, yellow school bus. This choice was probably a bad decision since people can bully me from the side, front, and back, but it's my spot. It's been that way since the first day of my freshman year, so I'm not changing it. People will bother me regardless of where I sit, and everyone who doesn't just plays games on their phones with wireless earbuds in. They don't care. They're in their own world. I stare out the window, watching the usual path of oak trees, yellowing grass, and two-story houses blur past, occasionally slowing as we come to various stops on poorly kept intersections.

A few stops in, an all too familiar body plops itself in the seat behind me. I sigh internally. This person was not someone I was looking forward to laying my eyes on again. Robert James Kurt. A sloppy, acne-ridden boy with messy red hair who is far crueler than he appears. I pretend not to notice him, but he knows me too well for that. This situation hasn't changed since before the 2010s. People love to bully me. Middle school was horrible enough, but I can't expect high school to be any different. Especially not with Robert around.

"Hey, long time no see. Huh, Emoly? Still wearing those dumb gloves?" Emoly. Emo Emily. He invented that last May. So creative.

"May I help you?" I reply.

"Aw, come on. Don't act like a stranger just because we haven't seen each other since the Spring."

Oh, no. He's probably going to do something now. The smirk on his face means he's thought of something.

Before I can react, he pulls the top of my hood down toward himself, almost choking me. I immediately try to unzip my hoodie, but of course, the old zipper gets stuck. I can still breathe, but the fabric and zipper are rubbing against my skin, making me panic more. It feels tighter and tighter.

"How could you forget about things like this?" Robert asks. Yep, I can't forget. Especially every time I've looked toward the front mirror, seeing the driver always more preoccupied with the route. If it's not loud on the bus, nothing happens.

I can't answer. I keep frantically fumbling with my jacket, but it's futile. All I'm doing is making it worse, the zipper pressing deeper into my neck. The bus finally makes an abrupt stop, my hood returns to me, and I can breathe. I preemptively unzip the jacket so Robert can't pull that trick again. It shows my chest a bit under my shirt, but I can zip it back up at school.

I continue looking out the window. Taking something out of my backpack to distract myself isn't an option. People here will steal anything. After being lost in thought over what just happened for a bit, a body comes and sits right next to me, making me flinch. Right. Corey and Zari come on the bus at this stop, and they've sat right near me. Corey is right next to me with his horrid breath, and Zari's in front of me. It's easy to tell they're twins—both blond, muscular, and cruel.

"Hey, heeeey, Emily!" Corey and Zari say together in the same mocking tone.

"Oh, your face is all red, and you're panting like a dog," says Corey.

"Get away," I growl through clenched teeth. Not a good idea, I realize.

"Oh, she is a dog. Growlin' like that," Zari says.

"Hey, Corey," Robert chimes in. "Do what she says."

This reaction must mean he has another trick up his sleeve. I can't trust Robert.

"Just sit next to me instead," he adds. I knew it. Classic. Now both Robert and Corey are behind me. My body is on high alert, and I can feel the adrenaline pumping.

I wait for inevitable torture, but nothing happens. Why haven't they done something yet? *Just hurry up. Choke me to death or do whatever you plan on doing.* I even catch myself involuntarily zipping my jacket up, hoping they might take the bait and get it over with. I am so anxious that I get into a fetal position to accelerate their reaction further. They oblige.

"Aww, Emoly, what's wrong?" Robert asks mockingly. "Upset nobody likes you? Are you gonna cry and cut yourself in the bathroom when we get to school?"

I don't do that, but I know they wouldn't care if I did. I keep my mouth shut.

"Ya, *Emoly*," Corey adds. "Gonna cut your wrist and *finally* die of blood loss? It would do us all a favor."

I sigh, getting up to sit properly in my seat, and keep looking forward. I focus on my breath and the back of the seat in front of me to calm me.

We haven't even gotten to school yet.

***

It's a good thing Robert's not that smart. He's not in any of my honors classes. However, Corey, Zari, and some other bottom feeders are. Despite what some people think, many teachers don't watch kids any more closely on the first day of school. It seems like some take a glance and make assumptions, especially here in Rosedale, so people are still able to torture me. Even lunch is stressful. I am in line for so long lunch ends before I can eat. The first day is always the time when the lunch period is the most inefficient. The upperclassmen aren't allowed to eat off campus until next week, so there are far more people than usual. At least I don't have to worry about finding a seat. I can't sit where I sat last year. I try not to think about that. It's not important—just some bad tables with even worse people.

The rest of school seems to be the same as always, except learning new information in a new grade. I think I would be much more enthusiastic about it if the money for this school went into teaching the subjects they require us to take to graduate instead of athletics and music. Sure, I like that the funding goes to the arts at all in the first place, but there can probably be a better balance. In the southern United

States, there is no way a school will lessen funding for athletics, especially football. It doesn't mean much for me to be doing high school choir, but being underprepared for college does. Rosedale is big on college too, so it seems ironic. Maybe they're making up for the lack of funding for the arts that occurred in my previous schools.

We have the usual antibullying assembly during the second half of eighth period, and I tune out most of it. It's the same thing every year. They exploit the story of some former kid who got bullied, tell everyone to think before they speak, and insist they can help if somebody is being bullied. It's all lies. I've never understood the "think before you speak" message for bullying anyway. I'm very certain people who call me names think about it and know exactly how I will feel. They just don't care. The administration is awful at addressing it too. All the schools I've been to so far are so focused on "getting the full story" and not being sued. "Zero tolerance," my ass.

After the school day finally ends, same as always, I walk around the building while waiting for my mom, who at least picks me up most of the time. I should be safe now. Robert, Corey, and Zari will probably take the bus home like they did last year. They're the only ones who bully me physically. Everything else is verbal or subtle, which I can deal with on some level.

After walking the halls for a while, I head outside toward the back of the school, hoping to avoid the trio if they happen to still be here. The back of the school has a large alcove that accommodates industrial equipment. I sit against the wall, placing my backpack in front of me and feeling the late-summer breeze. The various roars and hisses of the large machines are oddly calming. Maybe it's because the sound seems to go into the sky and follow the wind instead of staying here on the ground.

A hand comes from around the corner and plugs my nose. Another covers my mouth. I look up and see three people in front of me.

"Are you still not dead?"

Oh, no. Robert. Two new guys are with him, standing in front of me. Both are tall, one with a polo shirt and boat shoes, the other with black hair and a varsity jacket.

My heart is beating out of my chest. My lungs are frantic for air. When I try to breathe with my mouth, I only get Robert's sweaty palm. Licking his hand doesn't work; he doesn't budge. I can't move my head, either. I reach for Robert's arms and push, but they hold tighter. I kick, but Robert's coconspirators forcefully pin my legs. I keep trying to fight, making horrid noises I can't control as my body gives way to instinct. My fists clench the grass beneath me.

"Aw, look at you, struggling for air," Robert says. "I thought you wanted to die, Emoly. I'm doing you a favor."

I try my best to muster a glare. When he's focused on my eyes, I attempt to punch him, but my hand can't reach. I'm utterly helpless, and I hate it. I can barely see him through my watery eyes, and the world starts shifting. I keep struggling until I feel myself go weak.

2

COLE

———

Time for my first day at a new high school. I'm not sure how to feel yet. Everything seems so unfamiliar. I don't care much about what I wear or what kind of school supplies I have, but I am still unsure how people in Rosedale will see me. I have only known Plano. Luckily, my mom makes the same meal she does for every special occasion: homemade omelets with sopapillas. She doesn't have much time in the mornings to cook, so it's always nice when she does it. She knows how I like my omelets, and she gets up early to make the sopapillas from scratch. I think she feels bad I have to cook for myself most days. My grandparents have criticized her for it for a long time, which seems unfair considering it's just her and me at home.

As my mom and I pull up to the school, I am unsure what to think when I get out of the car and stand there in the breezeway.

"Have a great day, mijo!" my mom yells before speeding off to work. I am still surprised she has shifted her hours to drop me off at school. I continue standing in the breezeway and stare up at the building. The words "Rosedale Central" are set above the entrance in front of me. I didn't think

Rosedale schools would be so big. Even the elementary school further down the street would have been the size of my high school back in Plano. It feels surreal. However, I know I need to go inside, so I push open the glass door and enter a sea of activity. Students yelling, lockers slamming, and echoing feet rush into my ears in stark contrast to how quiet it was outside.

Upon first glance, this school seems more diverse than my last one. It was mainly white. It'll be refreshing to have exposure to more cultures. Hopefully, there are a good number of Latino students like me.

According to the school freshman packet, I'm supposed to wait in the gym before heading off to my first period. Only upperclassmen are allowed in the cafetorium at the center of the school, but luckily the gym is down the hallway from where I entered. After getting lost slightly where the hallway branches off, I reach the gym, and the echoing hubbub of all the other freshmen makes the cafetorium I passed by on my way here look like a ghost town. I have no idea where to go or what to do, so I sit against the wall and listen to a group of other freshmen talking about video games. I don't find a good time to join in.

To relieve some of my nerves, I recheck my schedule to make sure I remember where all my classes are and when I plan to switch out supplies in my locker. Then I look around the gym itself. A large painting on the wall opposite me depicts an angry gray rhinoceros with the words "Go Rosedale Central Rhinos!" painted below. There are also banners hanging from the ceiling showing what years they've won competitions in various sports. It's nothing exceptionally impressive, mainly local championships. The five-minute bell rings as I reached for my phone to check the time. That means it's time to go to my first class of the day. I hope I can just lie low for now.

My first period passes without incident, especially since seats are assigned anyway. The classrooms are similar to those in my old school, with the same fake-wood tables, uncomfortable chairs, and off-white walls. The familiarity makes me feel a little better, though. I expect English to be the same way, but my English teacher, Ms. Rowan, asks to talk to me at the end of second period. I couldn't have possibly done something wrong. All we did was write a paragraph about ourselves and what we liked about English as a subject. Afterward, it was reading time. Instead, Ms. Rowan asks me about speech contests. When my old school transferred my records here, they must have sent over my history of local speech contests as well. I was in them for a few years back in Plano.

"You know, Michael," Ms. Rowan tells me, adjusting her tortoiseshell glasses, "I read the get-to-know-you story you turned in for this period already, since you were one of the first people to turn yours in. Even in casual writing, you have a natural voice. Your vocabulary, punctuation use, syntax, and sentence structure are all unique and high-level. Have you considered doing writing contests again? I think you'd do very well."

"Oh, uh, thank you," I answer, caught off guard. "But I don't like writing contests anymore. I didn't like how competitive it got, and I got more into theater, anyway."

To my surprise, Ms. Rowan smiles. "I like that mindset." She continues, "You just want to make honest, original stories. I understand. Perhaps you'd consider publishing a story to some sort of publication, like a magazine? There are also many websites where you could publish them, but they won't get as much publicity. You could even publish a physical novel. There are no limits. I don't mean to pressure you, but you have so much talent as a writer. I like to help nurture talent and potential early on with my students."

I look at Ms. Rowan. She seems sincere, but my next period starts soon. Luckily, this is her off period, so nobody else sees me here. "I'll think about it," I say. "But you'll find out pretty quickly my stories don't have much depth. They're just fluff. I don't have much deep stuff to write about. I've had a pretty good life, and I don't really have strong feelings about any of it."

She looks at me weirdly. "Now, I'm not saying to become a pessimist," she warns, "but look realistically at yourself. I'm sure you have some deep emotions. Everyone does, especially teens. Some more than others, but try to explore yourself. Just don't let your emotions sit and rot. Express them in writing. That's how some of the best stories are made, and you'll feel better than you already do. But I digress. Let me know if you decide on anything, okay?"

"Okay," I agree with a small smile. She fills out a hall pass for me and lets me off with a wave, returning my smile. I head over to the gym for PE. This class is gigantic, and that's because some of the sophomores are in this class too, I quickly find out. The first thing I do is give my doctor's note to the PE coach. At least this part of my life hasn't changed. My asthma still makes me sit out of PE classes. It's a requirement, though, so I have to be here physically in some capacity.

"So, you can't do many activities?" she asks. "Don't worry. You're not the only one."

"Okay, thank you," I say, relieved she isn't some drill sergeant that would tell me to participate.

"Sure thing, Michael. Hey, do you prefer Mike?" I look at her and catch myself before I say no. Here, nobody knows me. I don't have to keep being Michael anymore. Even Ms. Rowan suggested exploring myself. I don't want to be Mike, though. That seems too rugged for me. Too close to Michael anyway. The second syllable. Cole. Yes, I'll be Cole. I like the sound of it.

"Actually, I prefer Cole," I reply.

"Alright, Cole. Feel free to sit in the bleachers to watch."

I put my stuff away in the small gym lockers and head to the bleachers. Not much happens, but I do notice very few girls are participating in the activities. Most of them are standing by the bleachers, talking to each other. Some seem to be teasing one tomboy that's playing the game, but that's about it. I'm surprised with how lax these coaches are. Maybe the girls are on athletic teams. My old school let athletes do whatever they wanted during PE. As the game goes on, they act as a cheer squad for a small group of guys. Their constant high-pitched praise makes my ears hurt.

At lunch, I get nervous about not having a place to sit in the loud, crowded cafetorium. I start looking for any sort of familiar face from this morning, and I soon spot a group of guys I recognize from the gym before school. They seem nice enough, and their table doesn't seem too chaotic. I nervously approach them, and somehow one of them recognizes me from the gym. He introduces himself as Andrew, and he immediately invites me to sit. That's a huge relief. We spend lunch talking about various things, including the video games I overheard them talking about this morning and how our classes have been so far. At some point, a sophomore named Robert gives us advice about some of the teachers. He seems to assume they are all horrible, though, so I don't take him too seriously. He seems like he just wants to brag a bit. He was nice enough to let me sit at the table, though, so he probably isn't a bad person.

Theater was the most interesting part of my school day. I'm glad this school has a theatre program so I can keep acting like I did back in Plano. The class involved a lot of moving around and improv games as icebreakers. I sat between two very enthusiastic best friends named Ana and Raina, and although I'm not annoyed or anything, their overwhelming energy makes it hard for me even start small talk with them. They do start some conversation with me, but I couldn't match their energy level. Luckily, they don't seem to mind. It was a fun time, and I think Ana and Raina will be willing to be friends with me.

The rest of the day is much less energized compared to PE, lunch, and theater, and I find myself looking at the clock, begging for the bell to ring. Does school end at 3:15 or 3:30 p.m.? I forgot, so I decide to try again to listen to my teacher explain math concepts I already know from eighth-grade math in Plano. It'll make time seem to go at least somewhat faster.

At 3:15 p.m., the bell rings, which is a relief. It may only be a fifteen-minute difference, but school ended sooner rather than later. My mom texts me that she is already outside, so I search for her car in the crowded parking lot, throw my backpack in the trunk, and jump into the passenger seat.

"Mijo, how was your first day?" she asks, enthusiastic as ever.

"Well, my teachers are all pretty great, and the classes seem fine. My English teacher was especially nice. She asked me about my speech contests after class."

"Que bueno, sounds like a good start," Mom replies. "Ah, did you give your gym teacher the doctor's note?"

"Sí, sí," I reply.

"She said it's all good?"

"Oh, no," I say, causing Mom to hit the brake. "Can I get my textbook? I left one in my locker."

"Dios mio, Michael, you're lucky we're still in the parking lot. Go get it before we leave."

I get out of the air-conditioned car, not fond of the outside heat wave, and luckily remember where the entrance closest to my locker is. I decide to explore a bit and go around the back of the school to get there.

Thanks to a lack of sidewalk, I go down the side street that runs directly behind the school, taking in the back of the building. It consists mainly of a grassy alcove with giant, noisy machines on either side. It seems like a nice hidden spot. I'm surprised I don't see any random druggies hanging about, but I guess I'm kind of relieved as well. The smoke would bother my lungs. That would be the last thing I need here.

I get to the entrance and soon find my locker. Not many people are still around. It's the quietest I've heard the building all day. Every noise I make with my locker echoes uncomfortably loud, so I grab my book as quickly and close my locker as slowly as possible.

I go back the way I came, making sure I didn't forget anything else. However, this time I notice someone in the grass by the machines. It's a girl in a black jacket, hugging her backpack, coughing and gasping pretty hard. I'm about to cross the street to ask if she's okay, but then I hear my mom honk. She can see me from where I am. I listen to the girl's coughs as I walk slowly on, and they get less severe, eventually, just her clearing her throat. *She's okay, then*, I assure myself, and hurry on to the car.

The whole way home the coughing bothers me. It was not normal. It wasn't an asthma attack. I would know. So at first,

I had thought it was an anxiety attack. That hadn't seemed right. Had she been choking and coughed something back up? No. I hadn't seen her with food or wrappers, either. No cigarettes, even. That leaves one idea that refuses to leave my head. She'd just been choked. Had a person choked her? Had she choked herself? There is something about her I can't quite pinpoint, and I feel obligated to find out.

3

EMILY

"So, did anything happen at school, Emily?" my mom asks.

"No, nothing other than normal first day stuff." My mouth feels dry and metallic. I hope it doesn't show in my voice.

"Did you tell any of your teachers you think you're a boy or some other weird thing? I don't need that this year. Had too many conferences last year and missed so much work."

"No, I didn't," I reply, trying to maintain my composure. She gets defensive at the slightest hint of tension in my voice.

Ever since I came out to her, she's been like a whole different mother. She basically ignores me.

For example, I haven't been out to shop for myself since then. When I ask, she just dismisses it and keeps on doing her business. My clothes, room decor, music, books, and even school supplies are from eighth grade and earlier or, in the case of school supplies, borrowed from others last year. Good thing I haven't grown, so my old clothes still fit fine.

Sometimes I wish I had another person in the house to counterbalance her attitude, but my Catholic Mexican dad would probably react even worse if he were here. I definitely don't want siblings, either. So, I'm stuck like this.

I even have to make myself dinner. She never makes anything for me or the both of us. I don't even get a say in what my mom buys, and she gets mad if I use the stove or oven. So it's just fruit, boxed foods, and microwave food for me.

Since my mom is in the living room, I eat upstairs in my bedroom. I have microwaveable cheese ravioli tonight with a glass of milk and old strawberries. Not an ideal pairing, I discover. Once done, I head back downstairs toward the back of the house to give my mom all the forms she has to sign for school. As soon as I approach, I can feel her aura of irritation.

"Ugh, all these forms," she groans, half-heartedly signing them without reading them. At least she did sign them. She got in trouble when she didn't last year. That was not a fun time.

***

My mom refuses to drive me to school because she doesn't see a reason to go out of her way, and I take the bus again. It seems weird my school isn't on her way to work but is on the way back, but maybe she's just making excuses. I look out the window as the bus follows the normal route, waiting in apprehension for Robert and the sicko twins.

"Hey, Emoly!" Robert greets me with a wicked grin. He then does something unusual and plops himself right next to me. I try to scoot to the side and kick at him, but he reaches around my head before I get to kick him. He now has me in a headlock, nice and low so the bus driver can't see from the mirror. He squeezes, and I can't move his arm. He's too strong. I can't throw him over my shoulder, either. The seat in front is in the way.

At the next stop, he lets me go, and I fall into the leg space between my seat and the next. Of course, I have to be small enough for this to happen. Corey and Zari laugh with Robert as they sit across the aisle from me. They throw taunts, but I barely register them and wait for my blood flow to return to normal. I get back into my seat and cradle the arm I fell on. My jacket is covered in random dirt and debris from the floor of the bus.

I enter school and head to the normal waiting area for the upperclassmen, which is the cafetorium in the center of the school. I get stares no matter where I look to sit, so I sit alone on some of the steps and see what's around me. I have a book with me, but it would get snatched and thrown if I read it here. Every so often, a jock passes by and pretends to be friendly, laughing to his friends immediately after, or someone slaps me with a laugh as they pass.

My first period is Spanish class, and we do speaking practices with the language lab. Cher, one of the girls who tormented me last year, is in that class, and she gives me weird looks the entire time. She also looks at her phone and back at me, giggling. It makes me super paranoid, so I check the bathroom before second period. I frantically examine my entire visible body until I finally realize. There are faded red marks on my neck from Robert. Not even that visible to me. Someone must have noticed and taken photos. Who could have done that, though, especially from a distance? Maybe it's footage of the incident instead? I quickly try to cover the marks with the hood as best I can, but it's no use, especially when I am about to change into gym clothes for PE.

I want to sit out today, and I have an excuse, thanks to Robert and his BS. However, my inner desire not to interact with the mean girls by the bleachers wins over as I am the only "girl" to get engaged in kickball. During PE, the coaches are always watching, so I don't get outright bullied here. I only get whispers from people behind me and on the sidelines, which I can handle. It's nothing compared to what I went through in middle school PE... I push that thought out of my mind. I need to stop ruminating over things that happened years ago. It seems so dumb. This isn't even the same gym. I haven't been to my middle school gym in over a year since I'm a sophomore now. I don't get myself sometimes. I need to play this kickball game.

At the end of class, Coach Naomi approaches me. I know what she's going to do. She attempted to make me do it last year too.

"Hey, Emily," she says with a hint of nervous energy in her voice. "I see you're still as athletic as ever! Are you sure you don't want to try out for the basketball or track teams this year?"

"No, sorry," I reply like I do every other time she's asked me this. "I just really don't have the time, and neither of those sports are ones I'm particularly passionate about."

Of course, I don't tell her the other reasons. First of all, I don't want to be on a girls' team, and second, the girls on those teams are like stereotypical cheerleaders. They're extremely cliquey and rude, and they don't like me *at all*. Plus, my mom probably wouldn't even spend evenings taking me to meets or practice. So, there.

Robert seems to have my schedule figured out, because he keeps passing me in the hallway and shouldering me into lockers, doors, and walls. Nobody else ever notices because he does it so discreetly that it just makes me look clumsy, which doesn't help things. I just hope he doesn't choke me again today.

The lunch line, once again, is full of hungry teens jumping the handrail and play-fighting each other in too small a space. I'm not the only one getting smashed into the wall by their antics. At this point nobody tries to stop it anymore. I can see one of the junior chemistry teachers just leaning against the wall on her phone. It takes almost fifteen of the thirty allotted lunch minutes to get through the line, but at least it's better than last time.

When I finally get through, I walk across a hall into the cafetorium. It quickly occurs to me I have no idea where to eat. I would sit alone, but the counselor would see me and try to talk to me. She does that with everyone who sits alone. I know it's her job, but I don't want that. I can't sit with students, either. Last year I sat with two different groups, and each one would harass me. I had only sat with them because one of the members claimed to like me. So much for that. One group had even soiled my fingerless gloves in tomato sauce. I had spent the rest of that lunch period washing them. I had to keep the wet gloves and my bare hands in my jacket pockets the rest of the day. I haven't been able to wear those gloves ever again.

Realizing I'm standing in the hall, I walk to the trash to dump my tray. It's a big waste of food, but I'm no longer hungry. Just thinking about last year's tables depresses me. It's not like I can give the food to some starving kid, so out it goes. I wander over to the bathroom since it's one of the few quiet places where I like to think. I enter and am disappointed to see Cher and her friend Lanie standing by the sinks. They look over at me. Cher pretends to hurl, and Lanie holds her neck and fakes choking. Before I can give them a disgusted look, Lanie says, "Oh, sorry. You're so disgusting, seeing you made us want to kill ourselves." She had a sickly grin on her face. She and Cher laugh and walk past me to leave, shoving me to the side and continuing to comment on their "hilarious" act. I groan and go into a stall and sit on the toilet, hunching over, so my arms rest on my legs.

I can't eat lunch in the bathroom. That much is obvious now. Lunch is when girls go to the restroom together. I'd be easily seen and even more harassed in a room where I can't escape. I'm technically not allowed to go to the library for lunch, but I wonder if I can sneak up there. The librarian wouldn't care, and teachers aren't really monitoring it anyway. I could try that now. I've got about ten minutes left of lunch.

I sneak up the stairs and look back to see if any teachers notice me. The library is down the all-white hall and to the right, and I enter. The large wooden door is louder than I expect, so I hold it and try to close it as slowly as possible, since the school has a huge echo. I look to the cluttered desk to the right and see that the librarian is in his natural habitat: attached to his computer screen in the back room. He won't say anything even if he notices.

I look toward the tables, and someone else is there. He's in my grade, but I'm not in any classes with him. I think his name's Trent or Tarian or something, but his last name is Kenji. His hair's red now; it was blue last year. His left side is still shaved, though, and he looks as cool with the old-school punk style as ever. He looks up at me, surprised, and then goes back to his book after a polite two-finger wave. I sit a few tables down from him and read my book. For once, I feel relaxed. The residual echoes of the cafetorium are minimal, the boy doesn't bother me the entire time, and I can read in peace. I decide this is how I will spend my lunch periods.

Just as I start a new chapter, the bell rings. My short moment of peace and quiet finished. How annoying; I have to go to precalculus now. I'm a grade ahead in math, so everyone else in the class is a junior. That doesn't go over well with them, since this is also an honors class. These juniors are the "smarter" ones, so their egos get bruised more easily. Not that I'm exactly one to talk. My academics are one of the few things I am confident in, so I am also guilty of basing self-worth on it. In the grand scheme of things, I just happen to get the information quicker than a lot of them. When we do review activities, I normally get an answer pretty fast, but the others have to spend time checking if I'm right. When the group is all guys, they'll ignore me and then come up with the same answer anyway. That sort of thing happens all too often with girls in my classes. I'm not a girl, but they certainly see me as one. Part of me wants to tell them to stop because I'm a boy, but another part of me knows even if I were a girl, it's not okay for them to do that.

After we rotate through all the activities, Mr. Sylvestro reviews the concepts more broadly and goes over some new terminology. Whenever he asks a question, I raise my hand, and I can feel the class take notice. Mr. Sylvestro doesn't seem to care, though. He calls on me regardless. I eventually stop putting my hand up due to anxiety, but it's hard to resist when he asks an advanced question. Nobody else knows it, so I nervously raise my hand.

He calls on me.

I get it right.

The kid behind me, Jack, just has to comment, "Well, *someone's* smart."

"I hope for the future of this planet and this species that it's not you."

Ah, shit. I didn't mean to say that. It just came out. Everyone laughs and yells, "Oooh, she got you!" I hope this Jack kid doesn't decide to take matters into his own hands later. I mean, he's a junior. He shouldn't care that much, right? He's got college prep to do anyway. It felt good, actually, but it still makes me nervous. Jack's glare isn't helping. Luckily, Mr. Silvestro calms everyone down without telling either of us to see him after class.

My mom running late to pick me up does have one advantage: it gives me time to walk around the school after hours. Walking through the halls after school is almost relaxing, if I could relax. The tap of my own shoes on the tile, the lack of other people, the eerie silence; it's nice for a change. It's one thing that's prevented me from absolutely hating the school. Being inside and visible seems like it would be better for me than being outside like the sitting duck I was yesterday. Nothing too bad can happen without somebody noticing. Maybe that's why I feel safer here.

Once I return home, I attempt to head straight to my room to work on homework. My mom seems to have other plans, though, since bills are due today. She forces me to stay downstairs while she rants loudly about her workday and, inevitably, all that she does for "the family." Comments such as "I slave every day to put a roof over our heads and pay the bills," and "It would be easier if I didn't have so many goddamn expenses" inevitably come up. She never says it out loud, but I always leave these conversations feeling like I'm the one who ruined everything for her. The conversation is never even about me, but she somehow ends up being the victim with me as a villain. She ended up stuck with me, but it's not like I asked to be born. She's the adult here.

When I can finally go upstairs, I pull up some anime and start some homework. Being productive can help in these situations sometimes. However, all it ends up doing is making me realize how lonely I am. I can't study with anyone, vent about my mom, or even talk to anybody when something exciting happens during the anime. Nobody would want to anyway. Not with someone as worthless as me.

4

COLE

As I walk around school today, I notice myself looking for the girl I saw behind the school. I consider asking Andrew since he's the only person I know so far, but I don't want him to think I'm creepy. I don't run into her before the first period, and I keep thinking about it during my first two classes.

When I get to PE, I have to change clothes even though I'm not even participating, and I take my spot on the cold metal bleachers. The coaches announce they're playing kick-ball today. I look for the girl from earlier, and I see her brown hair as she gets ready to kick. Thank God. She seems okay. I guess she's in my PE class, at least, so I can see her more. She kicks super well and even scores a grand slam. Nobody high fives her or anything, which I think is kind of odd since they do that with everyone else when they even make it to bases.

"Got your eye on that girl?" a voice whispers, almost making me jump out of my skin.

"What? No, I'm just watching the game," I insist, flustered. The boy who scared me stares, unconvinced, from under his red hair, which had fallen in front of his face. He's wearing an old band T-shirt with a denim vest covered in pins and patches. He also has straps attached to his pants. All he's missing from that punk look is a spiked mohawk and piercings. He's kind of scary looking, but there's also an innocence to it. He doesn't seem mean or dangerous in any way.

"Sure you are," he replies sarcastically. I'm about to defend myself again, but he changes the subject.

"What's your name, kid? I'm Trevor, the Asian punk. You also get to skip PE and watch amateur sports?"

I nod and reach out to shake his hand. "I'm Cole. Nice to meet you, Trevor. Asian punk?"

"Oh, you like shaking hands, huh? I prefer just waving, but I guess you'll be good when you get a job. Anyway, to answer your question, it's not every day you see some Asian punk, right? I'm the only one here I know of. Anyway, that's Emily. She's a sophomore like me. She keeps to herself, but she also gets bullied a lot. It was like this last year too. People here are cruel. I can't blame her for not wanting to be social. I don't want to interact with half of these people, either. I don't know her too well, but she seems like she could be cool."

"I told you, it's not about the girl."

"Then why'd you listen intently to everything I told you about her? Seems like a sign of interest to me."

I looked at him, impressed, but I wasn't about to tell him he was right. He probably knew it, anyway. People like that always do. I know he's just messing with me, though, so I let it go. It is nice to already be interacting like this with someone, even if he's just teasing me for now.

"If you want to talk to her, though," Trevor continues, "she seems very closed off. I wouldn't recommend it. Especially not out of the blue. Tread cautiously. You don't know what you don't know. I've heard some rumors, but I doubt they're true."

"Oh?" I pry, regretting it immediately. I don't want to participate in gossip, especially rumors. I look down a bit. Trevor sees my hesitation, nods, and doesn't elaborate.

We change the subject and get on the topic of our medical conditions since we're both sitting out. Trevor has a heart condition that used to be far worse than it is now; he'd spent a lot of time in the hospital in early elementary school.

He doesn't look frail, though. Sure, he's a bit skinnier than most, but it's not noticeable unless you're looking for it.

After a brief moment of awkward silence, he asks, "So, you like music?"

"Sure," I answer. I mean, I like theatrical soundtracks at least. But I have no idea if he's into that. He's into punk, metal, and some grunge. Basically, heavy rock, from what I can see.

"Well, do you have a favorite band?" I ask him. It's the only follow-up question I can think of.

"Actually, not really," he replies, looking up and touching his chin in thought. "I have a lot of bands I think are top tier, though. Some of the ones I mentioned earlier like System of an Up, The Fismits, Squarenuts, and the Dead Prezidentz have great lyrics and great riffs. I can't recommend them enough. Look at them if you want some first rate bands to check out."

"Oh, cool. I'll do that."

I now have some bands to look up this weekend. Normally I wouldn't do so. I'm not extremely interested in music. Ms. Rowan, though, really got me thinking about emotions, and rock music, like musical soundtracks, can be full of deep emotions.

As PE comes to an end, I look over at Emily again as she heads toward the locker room alone. The other girls go in groups with their friends. Her face doesn't give away any emotion. If Trevor notices me looking, he doesn't say anything. I follow him into the men's room to change into our regular clothes.

After lunch, I have my theater class, and today is significantly more active than yesterday. Ms. Castiel has us do all sorts of icebreaker games involving acting, dancing, and some miming. It's fun watching her demonstrate them all too. She definitely fits the stereotype of the eccentric drama teacher.

I'm also caught in some sort of crossfire between Ana and Raina, today because they have started to include me in all their conversations. My head moved back and forth so much I'm surprised I haven't pulled a muscle. I can't say I mind too much, but I am still not used to their energy. Their bubbly conversations at least bring action into the monotony of school like Trevor does.

Even more, I can't stop looking at Ana's hair. It's an afro in the back, but the front half of her hair is done in braids with colorful beads on the ends. I've never really seen a style like that before, but it looks good on her.

"I... I like your hair today, Ana," I tell her. "It suits you."

"See, Ana?" assures Raina, who is sporting the purple braided mohawk she had yesterday, "I told you I know what I'm doing!" She then turns to me. "I helped her with it last night. Thought it would help Ana be a little more confident."

"R-R-Raina!" Ana whines. "What are you doing? Oh, and thank you, Cole. You're one of the first guys to notice. Men are bad at noticing that sort of thing most of the time."

Ms. Castiel announces they're going to run a fall play, and my ears turn from Ana and Raina's discussion of hair to the actual class at hand. Ms. Castiel passes around an audition flyer, and the play will be the *Pied Paper of Hamelin.*

Man, that's a story I haven't heard for a while. It brings back a memory of my dad I had forgotten. I was pretty young, but I remember him telling me the "adult version" of the story. This version must be watered down: the children don't die, and the names of the children left behind are updated. Thinking about my dad makes my stomach hurt, so I stop. Better not to think about it. He left me, anyway, the *culo*.

"Hey, Cole!" Ana whispers, bringing me back to reality. "You're a freshman, right? Are you gonna audition?"

"Oh, well, I'm not sure. This is a bit sudden," I reply.

"Did you do theater in middle school?" Raina inquires. "Or would this be your first time acting? We can help you if it is."

"Ay no, I've done it before, but nothing major. I like acting, but I'm not the kind to go for a lead role."

"Yeah, well, with this white-ass play, neither Ana nor I could pull that off!" Raina exclaims. I'm amazed the theater teacher didn't hear her. I guess I should be equally disappointed the racism in casting would be that obvious.

"Well," I try to reassure them, "you all could be..."

"Trailblazers or something?" interrupts Raina. "No thanks, man. Not that type."

"Rainaaaa," groans Ana. "What's white about doing theater?"

"Um, girl, do you know the damn story?"

"No, but how *white* could it be?"

"So white, vampires would burn."

"Aww, really?"

"The entire story is about some pedo kidnapping children from some European countryside centuries ago. No melanin in sight, Ana."

I finally decide to interrupt with a joke. "I mean, don't we all have equal rights to be kidnapped by some flute player?"

Ana and Raina share a rare moment of silence, look at each other, and start laughing. I'm not sure if that went over well or not, until Ana playfully shoves my shoulder. I blush as she does it, but I try my best to hide it.

As I leave theater, Ana accidentally bumps into me by the front door.

"Oh my gosh, Cole, I'm so sorry!" she says. "Are you okay?"

"Yeah, I'm fine."

"Oh, good," Ana sighs as Raina tugs her arm to pull her away. "Raina, see you tomorrow!"

I continue out of the room, and I immediately run into Trevor, who has been leaning against a nearby wall. Did he wait for me?

"Your face is red," he notes with a grin. "Ha, just giving you a hard time. Oh, is that the audition page for the fall play? You gonna do it?"

"Trevor..." I mumble, still embarrassed he noticed me blushing. "This dumb play makes me think of my dad anyway. I don't know if I'm gonna audition."

"Well, Castiel does like to put her senior favorites in the lead roles," Trevor says. "But try not to let memories of your dad stop you from auditioning, whatever they are. The play could be fun."

"I'm surprised you're so supportive of high school theater," I counter. I thought punk people were against that sort of school involvement. Not to mention we've known each other for two days.

"I mean, as you said, it's high school theater. The politics are bullshit, but that's no reason to avoid it altogether. It's not like you're becoming a cop. I think you should audition. Even if to spite your dad a bit."

"Wait, you're not questioning the dad thing?" I ask.

This is the first time I've gone unquestioned after mentioning it to someone. I'm not even sure why I mentioned it to Trevor. Maybe because he's the best friend I've got so far.

"Why would I?" he replies casually. "It's none of my business. I know what it's like to have suboptimal family situations."

"Well, my mom is fine..." I clumsily defend. "My dad is a different story. He's not around. Like, I'm fine, but... you know."

"I do," he says. "I know what it's like to lose a parent, Cole. It's all good. The bell's gonna ring soon, but just know you can talk to me about that sort of thing if you ever need to."

Trevor starts to do a two-finger wave and turn away, but I quickly stall him for a bit longer.

"You've lost a parent too?" I ask.

"Oh, yeah," he replies. "Not my dad, though. My mom. She was the good parent, unfortunately."

"Oh..." is all I can think to say.

"Hey, don't worry about it. It was a long time ago," he reassures me. "Anyway, we should get to class. See ya!"

The pain in his face when he mentions his mom. Do I have that pain too, deep down, about my dad? I stand in the hall, stunned, as Trevor walks away.

5

EMILY

———

I'm going to do it. I'm going to sit at the back of the bus. It may normally be Robert's spot, but that's okay. Right? I need to protect my back, and I would never want to sit in the front of the bus. I don't want the driver seeing me. It's just embarrassing. Man, this is a crazy decision.

I had decided last night to sit in the back of the bus to prevent what's happened the past two days. I had a dream about it, actually. Maybe that's why I think I could possibly do this. I mean, what worse could he do? Maybe I know deep down this is a bad idea and just want to feel something. My brain is a confusing mush right now.

When Robert gets on the bus, it occurs to me the back seat can fit two people. Robert's certainly not going to let the backpack lying next to me stop him. My stomach drops. He sees me in his spot and gives me a glare. I try my best to give an equally intimidating glare, hoping my rising fear isn't visible.

"Emoly, how are ya?" he asks flatly, shoving my backpack off the seat and taking its place. I can hear my breath more as he squishes his body against mine, putting pressure on my torso. Oh god, why did I do this? I can't do anything now. The bus continues moving, and Robert continues to squish me between himself and the wall of the bus, which is not comfortable.

"Hello? I asked you a question, Emoly."

I can't speak. Anything I say will get me put through something worse. Even my rising heartbeat feels too loud.

"Hmm, fine then. Be like that. I'm just trying to be nice. Switch with me."

Robert squishes harder, so I lean forward to break free, and Robert slides into my old spot. The bus is moving, so I quickly sit on the end near the aisle. Looking up, I see Corey and Zari smirking in front of me. I turn around to look at Robert, who has been mouthing to them this whole time. When he sees me looking at him, he grins. I feel the bus taking a turn, and at that second, Robert shoves me into the aisle, facedown.

"Hey! Get back in your seat! Don't start exaggerating on the turns!" the bus driver yells as the rest of the bus starts to laugh.

"Yeah, go back to your seat, Emoly," Robert says as he carelessly throws my backpack over the seat in front of him.

After a few seconds, I push myself up and sit in my usual seat, hugging my backpack. I touch my forehead, and I can feel a bump forming. I must've bumped it on the metal seat legs. I immediately throw my hood over my head and pull the strings. I hope people won't notice this.

When I get to school, I run through the doors by the gym to reach the closest bathroom. There's a nice, pronounced bump on my head, almost like a broken off unicorn horn. I try to catch my breath, pushing my sweaty, numbing palms into the bathroom counter. I stare at my panicked face in the mirror, which scares me even more.

I hear the door start to creak, so I run into a stall. I try my best to keep my breath quiet by covering my mouth until whoever it is leaves, but it's so much harder when I'm hyperventilating. I can't make this stop. Even when the person leaves, I'm not any calmer, pathetically panicking in a bathroom stall. I'll probably die here, and nobody will notice. That's okay with me. The thought of running back into school with Robert feels like a pig to slaughter.

The ring of the morning school bell brings me back to reality a bit, and although it's not better yet, I can control my breath. As I get up, I vigorously shake my now-numb arms and legs to regain feeling. I try my best to breathe normally as I awkwardly trek toward first period.

In all my morning classes, people keep staring at me. My bump is covered, but I quickly realize my bus incident was recorded. Everybody knows, and I keep overhearing people watching it on their phones between classes. In PE, we play volleyball, and even I notice when people aim their spikes at me, they're aiming for my now-bare forehead. Maybe I'm just paranoid again.

Lunch provides some solace and peace after PE. I prefer the smell of books and the open-air feeling of the library to the crowded, stinky cafetorium. I eat upstairs again with that Trevor kid, and I make another bold choice of the day. I sit at the same table as him. I'm still shaken after this morning; I just need to be near someone. He looks up at me from his book briefly and nods in greeting before awkwardness forces both of us to look back down. I wonder if he understands.

I take out my lunch and realize Trevor doesn't have any food. It feels like it would be rude to eat in front of him without offering, so I place a bag of off-brand chips in the middle of the table. He looks up at me. I nod, and he takes the chips with a thankful smirk. Wow. He didn't even make a sarcastic comment. This could work.

"Dammit, Robert," I whisper to myself as I feel my forehead ache again. Dang, I said that out loud. Trevor doesn't show any indication he heard me, but I know he did. I look down at the snacks in my lap and start eating while reading, trying not to worry about the potential consequences of my words. I mean, if he's in here too, then who does he have to tell, right?

I spend precal dealing with occasional antics from Jack. Mostly glares, middle fingers, and snickers from him and his friends as they whisper about me. Nothing big. He even has the audacity to call me out in the hallway after class and asks me about my fingerless gloves in the middle of the hallway. It's simply weird. Is that really all he can tease me about? I look ahead and keep walking. He doesn't scare me. He seems to be all bark. I'm too tired to take him seriously anyway.

I will admit, I am proud of myself for being able to ignore him. He didn't even run and try to stop me. I walked away without anything else happening. That doesn't happen often.

At the very end of the day, I have choir. Normally, I don't think too much during it, since it's not an intensive class. However, today is the day they release the results of the vocal testing. Those with higher voices sing soprano, and those with lower ones sing alto. I've always been alto, so that's not what I'm waiting for. I'm waiting for new seating assignments. I would love to be in the back row, since whenever I am not the girly girls all seem to want to touch my hair without asking and ask weird questions about how I take care of it. I'm not entirely sure why, but they say it's super soft. I'm not sure how to feel about that. The only positive thing about it is they treat boys in my grade the same way. Not that the girls interact with me outside of this class. Maybe it's because this class is all girls, and there are no guys to spend energy on.

As Ms. Anker keeps assigning us to seats, I prepare to stand around for a while, since altos get their assignments after sopranos. Yet my time is far shorter than I imagined.

"At the end of the first row, for the sopranos, Emily."

Fuck.

***

Today I avoid looking directly at my mom, so she doesn't catch a glimpse of my bruise, which really isn't too different from the norm. I'm surprised I'm so self-conscious about it. She wouldn't care either way. I guess I want to spare a lecture, though. We go home in silence, listening to the radio station play ten minutes of ads. My mom doesn't bother changing the station. When we get home, I go straight to my room and lay on the floor, staring at the ceiling.

At night, Robert comes to my dreams. As do many other bullies I've known. I switch quickly between places I don't even recognize. No matter where I am, I try to hide from them as they talk about something I can't hear. I'm now at the school in the back area. I'm wrapped tightly from the neck down in white sheets. Robert is lifting me above his head through a crowd of all my enemies, who are holding torches and yelling, even though it's midday. I look up and see an old jacket on the wall. The sleeves are tied together over a large nail, making a nice hole. I freak out as I get carried closer to the pseudo-noose, realizing what's happening. They all loudly chant as Robert pushes me up until my head is as high as the jacket. I look through the hole at everyone. It's a cloudy night now, and I can't move. I scream, but it doesn't register with anyone. Robert moves his hands out from under my feet, and I snap awake as I fall into the noose, screaming.

"Shut up," my mom yells groggily. Guess I screamed as I woke. I'm sweating, and it takes me a few minutes to realize I'm alive and it was just a dream. I look at the time—1:30 a.m. I groan quietly and toss myself over. I can't sleep the rest of the night.

6

COLE

"Michael, despiértate! I have breakfast for us! And don't forget, Thursday is just the day before Friday!" my mom yells from the downstairs kitchen. I'm still groggy, but breakfast should help. She makes it sound like she cooked, but I know we have microwave pancakes waiting. That's definitely not bad, but the sounds of her cooking remind me of Abuela sometimes.

After breakfast we get ready, and my mom drives me to school again. As soon as I enter, I try to find Trevor, but he isn't around. I'm only allowed in the gym before classes start, anyway. I head over to sit with Andrew and the others, but the entire group stares at me as I approach.

"What?"

"Oh, nothing," Andrew replies. "We were just surprised you were here so early. Sorry if we freaked you out." His face gets more serious. "Do you know what happened with Robert? I saw him this morning, and he looked kind of scared. I asked him about it, and he wouldn't tell me what was up."

With Robert? Weird. Robert's a big guy. What could scare him?

"No, I haven't heard anything. That's surprising, though."

"Yeah."

We all moved on to talking about video games, and I'm still jealous because I don't have a console. I've only played on other people's consoles. I really want the BS8, but my mom has never said yes. I'd ask for my birthday or Christmas, but they're so far away. She also seems convinced all video games are inherently violent and will turn me into a gang member or something.

I meet up with Trevor in the locker room before PE. He tells me he did something good about some video of someone knocking Emily into the aisle of her school bus. I didn't know there was such a video, but then again, I don't really have people's contact information yet. Perhaps that's for the best in this case.

I make it to the bleachers before Trevor, and while I'm sitting I wonder why Trevor decided to do something about that video. It must be really bad if he cares about it that much. Does he feel the same pull I do to find out what's going on with her? It's only my first week of high school in Rosedale, and I'm already wrapped up in something like this. It's kind of weird. Trevor approaches with an oddly confident look on his face.

"What did you do?" I ask, nervous. The fact that he hasn't told me yet, combined with his face, is starting to make it seem like something scary happened.

"What I did isn't important," he replies mysteriously, looking ahead at the court. "But my suspicions were correct. I found out who was bullying Emily yesterday at lunch. I just happened to hear her whisper when she rubbed her forehead. It doesn't take a rocket scientist to put pieces together. I was suspecting the person, anyway."

"Who? And suspecting? How long have you been doing this?"

"I don't think I should tell you who it was, man. I don't want to give you information that could put you in a dangerous spot, especially seeing as you're new to everyone here. I, however, don't have much to lose. People know me and already have shitty opinions. I have a plan to get rid of this person. I'll tell you once this is all worked out. I've got this under control. So, what else is going on with you?"

"Oh, well..." I know Trevor's not going to continue on this subject without resistance, so I answer his question. "This morning, Andrew was talking about how this other kid in the group, Robert, looked freaked out. It was sort of weird, but they seemed really concerned. Hopefully I can ask him what's up at lunch."

"He's probably just got nerves. He's a freshie too, right? He might just be stressing over homework and all that."

"No, he's a sophomore, like you. He's Robert Kurt."

"Oh?" Trevor looks over at me sharply, wide-eyed. He tries to look calm, but I can still see the tension in his arms. Why did he get so tense? Robert seems like a nice person, even if he is a little crass.

"Do you know him?" I ask innocently, pretending to ignore Trevor's body language. It feels uncomfortable that he's not as confident as he's been before. It feels like I've hit a sore spot somehow.

"Yeah, I've heard of him," Trevor replies. "He's definitely got a reputation behind him. Are you friends with him?"

"He hasn't said so, but we sit together at lunch and in the morning with Andrew's crew. He talks to me and stuff, so I think he likes me, at least."

"Well, I guess that means you don't have to worry about being on his bad side."

Wait a minute… how did I not get this before? Trevor doing something bad, Emily's attacker, Robert freaking out, Trevor's body language at the mention of him being my friend and what he just said, could it be…?

"Trevor. Be honest with me."

"I normally try to be, so go ahead."

"It… was Robert, wasn't it? Robert attacked Emily. He must've been the one who shoved her. It's no coincidence you do something, and the next day people are telling me he's freaked out over something."

Trevor sighs and looks down at his knees, then looks me straight in the eyes. "Damn, you've got a good brain. I hoped to keep it from you for your protection initially, but so much for that since you know him personally. At least you are on his good side. Yes, it was Robert. Don't tell anyone, though, especially him. Don't even act differently around him. If he doesn't think you're involved, he won't hurt you. If he does, tell me."

I stare at Trevor. I don't know how to reply to that. Would Robert hurt me? He didn't seem too bad when he was with me. Would Robert hurt me if he found out? What the heck is this town? Nothing like this happened in Plano. I decide not to ask Trevor any of those questions.

Lunchtime brings me back to a feeling of normalcy. Sitting at a lunch table with people I know talking about random things is as normal as you can get. I'm not even sure what they're talking about. I'm not paying attention. I'm soaking in the whole scene, noticing they look like a bunch of extras in a high school film. Maybe this school is a film somehow. Maybe the truth is just weirder than fiction.

Suddenly, someone grips my shoulder from behind. I snap my head around to see who it is.

"Yes, oh!" I try not to show I know anything about Robert as I come face-to-face with him. Everyone else greets him warmly.

"Ha ha. Sorry, Robert, you surprised me."

"Aw, it's no problem, Cole," Robert replies. "Wanna come with me for a second? I have to talk to you in private."

I look over at Andrew, who also seems confused but not particularly disturbed. The others have already gone back to their conversation. Robert is not removing his grip, and I can't act like I'm suspicious of him. I agree to go with Robert, and he takes me to an empty hallway on the other side of the cafeteria. My stomach starts to churn in dread, but I remind myself there's no way Robert knows I know anything. He probably doesn't even know Trevor and I know each other. I keep playing these reminders in my head as Robert stops and faces me.

"So, Cole," he starts, "why do you hang out with us?"

He has a grin on his face like Trevor did this morning. Did he also do something?

"What do you mean?" I ask. "You all seemed okay with me on my first day, and I sort of know Andrew at this point. Nobody else has really asked me to hang out with them yet."

"Oh man, you're playing dumb with me, huh?" he whispers, returning the grip to my shoulder. "You think I don't see you and your little boyfriend Trevor hanging out together? Conspiring against my back?"

"What?"

Robert looks around and then locks eyes with me again.

"Okay, buddy, lemme tell you something," he continues. "You see, yesterday morning those same bros and I were messing with this one girl. We were just messing with her, really, but yesterday after school, Trevor walks up to my bros and me. Did you know this?"

"No! I wasn't part of this!" I insist.

I flinch as Robert's hand shoves further into my shoulder. He doesn't believe me. I shut my mouth, and he continues.

"He threatened us and told us he would send that video all over if we didn't stop messing with her. I kept telling him it wasn't a big deal, but he kept at it. He was just savage, kid. It was in his little eyes too. He's insane, probably because there's no brain in the skull of his. Or because his mommy died, and now he's all emo. Luckily for me, he can take punches."

This is Robert...? Oh my god. This is why Trevor was so tense. I can't even begin to refute all of the offensive things he's said so far since he keeps going.

"That video can't fall into the wrong hands. It doesn't look good at all. If it goes out, who knows how people will interpret it? I would miss messing with someone, though. It made the days less boring, you know? So, if I can't mess with Emily anymore, I need someone else. You know? I also need to make sure your little beaner mouth doesn't go spreading this info to everyone. So, this works out, huh? I want to see if you can take a punch too, *friend.*"

I see a gleam in his eye, but I have no time to react before he sucker punches me right in the stomach, completely winding me. I collapse onto my knees, gasping for air. Robert looks at me with puppy eyes and acts like he has no idea why I'm on the ground. I can't even glare at him. Wait, this isn't good. I can't get my breath back. *Pinche pendejo.* He's walked away, so I quickly pull out my inhaler and try my best to regain my pained breath. Once I can finally breathe on my own, I head back to the cafetorium, but it seems like the next lunch period started. I didn't even hear the bell.

Lunch may not have been the return to normalcy I was expecting, but I hope theater class goes well despite my unexpected tardiness. I want to forget what just happened so bad, even if my stomach won't let me. I feel nauseous. If anything, this is good acting practice.

I try to act normal in theater, and luckily the class is less physically involved today. Exercise would have probably made me vomit. Ana and Raina are so busy with their own conversations they don't notice anything off about me. This period does feel like a normal class. Nothing strange going on. Just me from the outside looking in at the monotony I suddenly crave. Afterward, Trevor is standing across the hall from the door, just like before. I don't know what to say after hearing what happened between him and Robert. I look at him and hope he talks.

"Hey, Cole," he says. "Still worn out from sitting on the bleachers like a couch potato?"

"Huh?" I sigh.

"You're sweating," he remarks. "Did you all exercise in theater or something?" I have to lie. He can't know what Robert did to me. What if I ruin his plan somehow? I don't want him to have to worry about me too.

"Yeah," I reply, still slightly breathy. "We did a lot of choreography stuff for the play." Wait. That doesn't happen until after at least the auditions. I hope he doesn't know enough about theater to take that into account. I'm not great at coming up with things on the spot. Unfortunately for me, Trevor catches on. I see it on his face.

"Cole, I'm fine with many things. Bullshit is not one of them. It's that simple. You don't have to tell me what's going on, although I want to know. If you don't want to tell, just say so. Don't pathetically lie to me. There are too many liars running this world." He looks at my stomach, and I realize I'm still holding it and take my hand away. It makes me more nauseous.

"Did something happen, Cole?" Even though he gives me a knowing look, I can't tell him what Robert did. I'm not ready.

"Not really," I finally answer.

Trevor turns and walks away with his sharp words regarding my lie repeating in my head. Robert's words also loop as I watch Trevor leave. How could Robert say those things about Trevor? Should I tell Trevor what Robert said? Does Trevor know what happened to me? How could he?

I sigh and head to my next class, hoping to hide all of this. At first, I was slightly concerned about Emily, but now I'm concerned for my own safety. I'll wait and see how it plays out. I feel like this should be a bigger deal to me. I mean, Robert just did what he did. I've already forgotten what it was, though. I know he socked me in the stomach, but I don't have much memory of it now. Maybe that's what I do to avoid deep emotions? I forget? It seems right...

7

EMILY

It's finally Friday. This first week of school has felt painstakingly long. Luckily, today is the first meeting of the anime club, and I'm starting my new position as the sophomore representative. Honestly, the anime club is one of the few things I like about this school. I'm not super close to anyone, but it's nice to be around people who don't actively hate me. Somehow, the members like seeing me as an authority as a grade-level representative. Luckily, the position is not elected. I wouldn't be here if it were. Their insistence on calling the reps "senpai," which means "upperclassman" in Japanese, is surprisingly strong, but they're technically using the word right, at least. I'm going to go over that during the meeting today.

I sit in my normal seat on the bus again today, not wanting a repeat of Wednesday. I endure the usual taunts along with my newest one, "goblin girl," from the purple bump on my head, which unfortunately is still visible from a short distance. There's apparently a video of my incident going around, so this will last longer than my injury. At this point, I'd rather hear "goblin boy." Oddly enough, the "girl" part bothers me more. I haven't had the energy to shower in a few days, so I feel enough like a goblin anyway. I stick out more than I would like.

Being called a girl also makes me hyperaware of my body, even though I'm wearing my hoodie. I find myself pulling on the fabric in front of my chest more than usual. Man, even backpacks make it seem obvious I have boobs. They're not big by any means, but even the baggiest hoodie wouldn't hide them. Clothes are normally big on me anyway, since I'm so short. Somehow, no clothes, no matter how they are sized, will hide my feminine body.

I endure the usual beginning of the day, getting a note thrown at my head that reads "Dyke" for absolutely free, no money down, and I go to my peaceful refuge at lunch. I haven't seen Robert all morning, and word in the girls' locker room during PE is that he skipped. I've never understood that. Why bother taking the bus to school if you're going to leave? It works out for me, though, so I don't question it again.

After fighting my way through the lunch line, I recycle the inaccurate note, leave the cafeteria, and head up to the library with my food. I place my chips on the table again, and Trevor thanks me before taking them and returning his focus to his book. Hmm, a horror novel. I think to ask him about it, but I'm not comfortable talking with him much yet. I have to study for my precalculus test next period. Who gives a full test in the first week?

After I've studied for a while, I notice my plate is empty while Trevor is still eating chips. He eats them so slowly too. It's like he's savoring them, which is weird for potato chips. My curiosity gets the better of me, so I ask, "Why are you eating the chips that slowly? Are they that good?"

Trevor looks up at me with a surprised look on his face. Am I too direct? Was that weird to ask? He looks for a little longer and finally replies.

"Huh?"

"Why do you eat them so slowly?" He gives me a weird look, and I get nervous. "I mean, I'm curious, because I don't see people savor junk food like potato chips."

"Well," he starts, "do you see me with other food?"

"Well, no..."

"That's why I savor them. It's all I eat for lunch. School food sucks ass, and I don't bother bringing anything from home. So don't stop bringing stuff." He winks with a smirk and goes back to eating his chips when I go back to reading. I guess no other questions, then. I can tell he didn't tell me the whole story. It's written all over his body language. He keeps looking around awkwardly and starts spacing. How can I expect him to tell me everything anyway? We barely know each other. I should focus on precal anyway.

I'm the first to finish my test in class today, and I feel the usual stares from the rest of the class as I stand to turn it in. However, this time I also feel Jack's gaze burning into the back of my head. I'm facing the teacher and hand in my test with one hand. I use the other to flip him off behind my back. I immediately regret it and worry Jack will comment, and I'll get in trouble. He makes a noise like a "hey," but Mr. Sylvestro tells him to be quiet. That's it. Lucky me. I even see some indirect smirks from people who were aware of what I did.

Jack comes up to me after class, and I glare as soon as he does. He first tries to shove me and then spews some bullshit about how he hates me or whatever. I don't feel like listening too much. For some reason, he's oddly preoccupied with asking me how my hands look under my fingerless gloves. After having gotten away with flipping him off, it is hard to take him seriously. I then realize I shouldn't take him seriously and stop trying. I look at him and walk off. Luckily, he doesn't follow me. I bet he looks like an idiot right now. That was a power move.

In choir, I still hear murmurs about me being a goblin or a witch, but at least it means they're not treating me like I'm some zoo animal like they usually do. However, I am still singing soprano, and I hate it. I miss singing the lower parts of songs. It made me feel much more powerful and masculine. Almost like I could have belonged in the men's choir if not for my sex. My voice can be lower than all the others, so why do I have to sing all feminine? This doesn't feel fair. As an alto, I could at least pretend I was a high tenor or something.

My English teacher is having reading-time Fridays like my teacher last year did, ending my day on a quieter note. It's such a relief to know I'll still have this time every Friday at 2:30 in the afternoon, just before school ends for the weekend. I soak the calmness in slowly, savoring it like Trevor with his chips. The smell of old books on the shelf in the classroom also adds to the aesthetic. I know the quiet is about to end.

After school, I head over to Ms. Simpson's classroom to help with preparations for the anime club. On the way, the loud clamor of voices guides me to the hall in the back of the second floor lined with members waiting to enter. After most of the students have already left, the club's commotion stands out and continues echoing as infamously as ever throughout the second floor. Teachers have complained in the past. I look at the line, and I see a good mix of familiar and new faces. They've got their cosplay accessories, stuffed animals, and volumes of manga out and ready, sharing them with their friends. It is nice to see these kids unmasking, so to speak. I'm glad they have that, even if I don't. I have missed constantly having to make them quiet down for some reason.

Once everyone enters and the meeting starts, we let all the freshmen and other new members introduce themselves.

We ask for their name, favorite anime, and a fun fact. All the new members seem pretty great, but one stands out in particular.

"Hey, everyone," he says, shoving his hands in his pockets and shuffling his feet. "My name's Cole. I just moved here, and I thought the club poster downstairs looked interesting. I don't know any anime or comics or anything like that. A fun fact is I'm bilingual—English and Spanish."

It's unusual to have a new member who has had no exposure to anime or manga, and he's Hispanic! There aren't too many Hispanics in this school, surprisingly. Although, I'm not sure if they'd count a half-Mexican like me if there were such a group. This guy does seem nice, though. Maybe if I get to know him, he can teach me some culture. Growing up with my super white and non-Hispanic mom didn't allow for that, but at least it means I didn't have to have a quince last year. Dresses are not for me, especially fancy quince dresses. That doesn't mean I don't want to experience other parts of the Hispanic side of my culture, though.

After the introductions, we discuss some logistical things and the meeting format. The part everyone is waiting for, though, is voting on an anime to watch this year. Ms. Simpson likes expanding our tastes, as she puts it, so we can choose from some more niche options.

I've already seen *Other*, but it ends up being the winner. When figuring out where to sit, I feel the same fear I did on the first day of school when looking into the cafeteria. Where do I sit? While scanning the room, I notice that Cole kid sitting in the back of the room by himself, and I can't help but feel for him. I decide to sit next to him, and we both watch together as the lights turn off and the projector begins to flash.

8

COLE

—

Well, my first week of school in a new town was interesting. Is it normal for places to be as crazy as this? No, there's no way being socked in the gut within the first week is normal. Trevor is not normal, and neither is this plan of his to help Emily. He's pretty much blackmailing Robert. I don't know how he can do that with Robert being so much scarier. It must be good blackmail.

When I get to school, I look around for club posters. I agreed to be in the play, but my mom said I needed more clubs to impress colleges. I haven't even thought that far yet. She wants me to be involved. That was part of our reason for moving here.

While looking around at clubs like journalism, Spanish (um, no thanks), French, robotics, and other academic clubs, I stop in front of a poster by the water fountains that catches my eye.

It has hand-drawn cartoon characters in a familiar style. It's Japanese, I think? Sure enough, the top of the poster reads: *Rosedale Central High School Anime Club*. Anime, huh? I remember reading the comic versions before in the Plano libraries, but I haven't done it in a while. This club sounds more interesting than all the academic ones, so maybe I'll go to the first meeting, which is—I scan the poster to find the meeting date—later today. That was fast. It will make my mom happy to see me getting on it right away, at least. I text her to pick me up when the meeting ends, and she replies cheerfully and tells me to have fun. I should be grateful that she doesn't decide my clubs for me.

I've been worried about seeing Robert, but I've yet to see him before PE, which is promising. Trevor confirms Robert's absence for me in PE while we're sitting on the bleachers. I still feel bad about lying to Trevor, since he seemed upset by it, so I finally explain what happened with Robert yesterday. Trevor's eyes widen, and he looks worried. I hope this wasn't a mistake, but I'm hoping Trevor can protect me too.

"Look, Cole, I know Emily is not the only person Robert bullies," he says. "She has been in the most danger, as far as I know. Stopping Robert is good for all of us, and him going to you instead proves he won't stop going after people."

"Why can't you report him?" I ask. "Why is this whole blackmail plan of yours necessary?"

"I don't trust this school to do anything with regards to bullying," he replies. "Robert has no weapons and can play everything off as an accident. My experience with school discipline has always involved some sort of victim-blaming. As an outsider to the situation, I won't subject Emily to that bullshit. The school must play a 'neutral' card as if both people are in the wrong. It's state law. I don't know how your old school was, but here in Rosedale, that's how it is. It's all performative. That's why it's necessary. This isn't just about Emily."

"I thought Emily was the whole reason we were doing this, though..."

"No, we're doing it because it's the right thing to do. Emily, and now you too, finally gave me the push I needed to act. I should have done this last year, Cole, when I was a freshie like you."

I want to ask Trevor more, but I don't know what I'm supposed to say. Maybe I don't understand Rosedale enough. Sure, I've had rude or racist teachers before, but I guess I thought Rosedale would be better since it's more diverse and seems wealthier. Maybe that means I really should watch my back if things aren't that different. Now that I think about it, Robert did call me a beaner. Is that sort of thing normal here? Everyone else has been nice so far. It seems like Robert is just always mean, though.

At lunch, everything goes as normal, making it through the line and sitting with Andrew's friends, without Robert. Of course, that's a relief to me. I don't talk much; instead, stuffing myself with food while thinking about Trevor's plan and Robert's threat yesterday. I haven't had to use my inhaler for a while, but I needed it because he winded me so bad. I really hope he didn't see it. I don't want to be known as "that kid with asthma" again.

As soon as I walk into the theater room behind the stage, Ana and Raina yell my name, snapping me out of my thoughts. I run to my seat as everyone's eyes turn toward the three of us. Luckily, they go back to their business as soon as I sit down.

"Cole," Ana starts, lowering her voice, "do you know Senorita Pasvar?"

"Um, no?"

"The Spanish teacher!" Raina adds.

"I don't take Spanish. I thought you both knew I was fluent."

"Duh, we know that, Cole. But do you and her talk or anything?"

"Why would I?"

"Raina!" Ana growls.

"Oh, that didn't come out right. I'm sorry, Cole."

"Um, you're fine. Why do you ask?"

"She helps Ms. Castiel a lot with the semester plays. She's cool and very proudly Dominican. She's older, but Ana and I like her a lot. She seems to have a better grasp on the world than most of the teachers here."

"Oh, um, cool," I reply, unsure of how to respond.

"Yeah!" Ana adds. "And she brings these jelly turnover things to rehearsals a lot!"

Ana's smile makes my stomach feel weird, but in a good way. Could she like me? It felt a little flirtatious, but maybe that's just me being hopeful.

After my last period of the day, I meet up with Trevor by the theater room. After usual greetings, he asks if I have plans for the weekend, so I tell him I'm going to the anime club meeting today. I don't actually know what my mom has planned, but there is probably a lot of shopping and cooking involved, since we just moved in.

"Do you want to come with me, Trevor?"

"Man, I wish I could," Trevor replies. "But I don't have time for clubs and stuff. I have to be back home early to help around the house, and my old man gets really mad if I'm late."

"Oh, that's too bad. It would be cool to be in a club together."

"Yeah, it would be. Have fun. I gotta head home. Oh wait, here."

Trevor hands me a piece of paper with an email address on it.

"I don't have a phone," he explains. "We can use this to message each other. Send me a test email this weekend, and I'll get back to you to confirm it. See ya!"

With another two-finger wave, he speed walks out of the school exit. Guess he really does have to be home. With nothing else to do now, I put the paper in my backpack and head upstairs to the club room.

I can't find the room, but I hear a loud group and head in that direction, hoping maybe it's the club or someone who may know where the club is. Once I reach that hall, though, I can immediately tell I'm in the right place. There is a huge line stretching out across the hallway, and the clamor increases as I join them. A good amount of the members in line are in costume and have stuffed animals and comics. It's a completely different vibe from how people are during school, but it's nice they can bring what they like here.

Emily is here too, looking brighter than I've ever seen her.

I didn't know she already liked this stuff. It seems odd to me to see her happy, but it's a good thing. Maybe we can get to know each other better. Once the club starts, the line moves so quickly I don't get a chance to say hi to Emily on my way into the classroom. I barely have time to examine the room before I hear the booming voice of a teacher.

"Hey, everyone, I know you're excited, but sit down! We have to get started quickly! And be quiet. We don't want to have a repeat of last year, do we?"

"No, Ms. Simpson!" yell the upperclassmen as people quickly move to tables with their friends. I can't figure out where to sit, so I go to an empty table in the back. I'm just observing the club at this point anyway. The noise and chaos are already making me more nervous.

Emily and the other grade-level representatives start by having us all introduce ourselves. I'm not scared to do so, but I still have no idea what any of this is. I thought I'd be more nervous during my introduction, but it went okay. I got some smiles from other members and nice applause. These people seem accepting.

I stay out of voting for an anime to watch, because I don't even know the first thing about what's good or not. The titles and trailers are confusing, but I like the art and am interested in some of the options. The one the club votes on is a show called *Other*. I'm not used to horror, but the animation and acting in the ad are impressive. Emily seems excited about it too, from how she keeps trying to explain the plot to me.

Surprisingly, Emily sits next to me during the anime viewing, but it's oddly comforting. I can't find any words to say to her during the episode, but she doesn't say anything either. There's just a pleasant aura as we take it in, and it makes me wonder if she somehow recognizes me as someone in her gym class. I'm not sure why she'd have any reason to recognize me, though. It's probably just a coincidence. She may not know it, but I do feel a sort of connection now that we've both had to deal with Robert. I hope both of us end up safe.

9

COLE

———

A silhouette pins me against a wall, almost like Robert did on Thursday. Well, the shadow must be Robert, right? Who else could it be? I try to resist, but I feel like a child pinned by an adult. It's impossible. I close my eyes to try to figure out if I'm dreaming. I open my eyes, and suddenly the wall behind me has become a floor, the silhouette pinning me from above. I can't make out its face in the dark, and I still can't tell if it's a dream. As I look over at my arms, I realize I am a child. Suddenly, the pain starts. I can't figure out where it's coming from, but it's a pain that moves all over as if the shadow was pain itself. The dream keeps trying to tell me who this shadow is, but I won't believe it. I can't believe it.

I wake up on Saturday completely unprepared for the day ahead.

It turns out my mom will have the whole family over for a housewarming party, and she hadn't bothered to tell me until last night. I don't mind my abuelos and primos coming over, but it's a marked shift from the quiet weekend I was expecting.

We all make tamales together, which makes my arms surprisingly sore even after just an hour. I mostly keep to myself and try to keep track of all the conversations going on around me. At least six conversations were going on at any time, in Spanish and English, but luckily I'm not in the loud kitchen for the entirety of the day.

Our family has an extremely specific recipe, so I soon end up helping look after my primos Mateo and Carla too, who Abuela says aren't old enough to properly help make them yet. She's probably not wrong. They're only seven and nine years old, and Abuela is picky. Even earlier, Abuela constantly critiques my chicken stripping technique.

Wanting some relief from the steam and noise inside the house, I bring Mateo and Carla outside. They like playing tag with each other, so I sit back in one of the cloth patio chairs and make sure they don't hurt themselves.

"Miguel, Miguel!" Carla yells after some time. "Do you want to play adventurer with us? Mateo said we need an expe-exidi-exi... well, a group leader!"

Adventurer is a game Mateo and Carla like to play with each other where they pretend they are researchers in a rainforest making discoveries.

"An expedition leader?" I ask. Carla's eyes light up in recognition.

"Yes, yes! One of those! Since you're the oldest and you do acting stuff, you should do it."

"Okay, sure, Carla. I'd like to play. It will help me practice my acting too, so thank you for inviting me."

She smiles and happily claps as I walk over to them, and while Mateo isn't quite as expressive, he's very protective of Carla and seems happy because she is. She lucked out with having that kind of older brother. If someone like Robert bullied her, Mateo would have fought him the day after. He'd gotten in trouble for that sort of thing before.

I try not to think about Robert anymore and get into my new role as an expedition leader in their imaginary rainforest. It's easier to play a role when the real me feels like it's pushed somewhere else, escaping from reality for a bit. That's why I like acting so much, even just for a kid's game.

I may not have gotten much sleep this weekend, especially since that nightmare keeps repeating every night, but I certainly got a full stomach of good food. That's got to count for something.

When I head down for breakfast on Monday, I get some cereal for myself, and my mom insists I take a few of the tamales with me.

"Mami, por favor..." I plead with her. I just want to eat my cereal right now.

"Hacemos estos como una familia y algunos de estos están para dar a tus amigos nuevos."

She insists I bring them since we made them as a family, and part of the intention was to give some of them to my new friends. I guess I have no other objections, so I quickly give in. I must just be cranky from lack of sleep.

"Okay, okay, está bien, no necesito mas."

It quickly occurs to me that Ana and Raina wouldn't mind trying a tamale, right? They seem interested in Mexican stuff, at least with language. Ana may really like it, as would Raina, of course. Maybe Ana will smile again. I ask my mom for two more tamales, which seems to make her happy. She gives me four in case I get hungry. I guess I could give some to Trevor or Andrew too.

When I reach the entrance to the gym, I see Robert talking with the usual group. Just seeing him reminds me of that punch. I decide to back away slowly as if he were a bear, but he notices me. The moment we make eye contact, I feel my stomach drop. He hasn't forgotten. My dream flashes in my brain, and I run toward the bathroom on the furthest end of the building, hoping I can lose him and hide. Luckily, nobody is inside, so I run into the stall and stay as still as possible.

I hear the door slam open a few seconds later.

"Oh, Cole, I know you're here."

My stall is one of two, so he reaches me in no time.

"You thought you'd lose me here? That's pathetic. You're even hiding in the disabled stall? Why? Are you retarded or something? Then again, y'all Mexicans can only water my plants anyway. Maybe that's why you think you and your family of illegals can move here."

"Dude, what is wrong with you?" I shout. "Why the hell are you so ignorant?"

"Ignorant? Who's more ignorant: me, who has types like you, Emily, and Trevor all figured out? Or is it you, a pathetic little beaner who runs to the disabled stall and can't mind his own business? Your father must be so embarrassed."

I know he's trying to upset me, but I still can't help feeling tears of frustration.

"I don't have a dad! Get your facts straight!"

"Ah, just like Emily, huh? Trevor doesn't have both parents, either. His mom's dead. Y'all kids are all the same: left weak and vulnerable because your parents never loved you. Why would they? I will admit, though, it's nice to see you try to fight back. Let's see how well you do."

Suddenly, I feel a strong kick in my torso that knocks me against the wall. When I regain my composure, Robert has my backpack in his hands with a grin on his face. A wave of fear hits me again, and I just stand there, trying to catch my breath.

"You should know better than to leave your things on the floor, Cole. Do you know why?"

Robert then proceeds to unzip my backpack, dumping all of my notebooks, folders, and my lunchbox with the tamales on the floor of the bathroom before throwing it to the side. "Oh, what have we here? What does Cole bring for lunch, I wonder? Tamales? Just a bunch of tortillas? Drugs, perhaps?"

I'm still frozen in fear as Robert opens the box and laughs at the fact it only has the tamales in it.

"You know, Cole, you've gone all silent now. Do you want me to take your tamales? Y'all do make good food. Hmm, maybe I'll just take one."

"No!" I yell suddenly. I just want whatever's happening to stop. "Why are you doing this?"

"Because I need some outlet. Since your little friend Trevor blackmailed me, I can't touch Emily. Imagine how he'll feel if he found out about you and me. It'd be real embarrassing for him, huh? Acting like some sort of Batman but just making things worse. He won't save you. He can't. He'd hate you if you told him. You know what, let me see one of these tamales of yours."

He picks up one tamale and then drops the lunchbox on the floor with a loud clang. He bites into it, and then he throws it on the floor.

"I can taste your weakness in it. Pick this up yourself, you dog. Consider this a warning. I can and will do much worse, especially if you tell. If you want to keep Emily safe and keep Trevor as your little friend, you can't say shit."

With that, he finally leaves, but I still can't move, even after the door shuts. I look at the pile before me. I slowly walk over so I can see the contents of the lunchbox, and, to my relief, the other three tamales survived. My folders and notebooks seem to be in order too. I guess I'm lucky it's only the second week of school; there's not a lot of work in those folders yet.

In PE, I want so badly not to think about this morning that I ask Trevor something I figure will keep him talking: how he got into punk rock music.

"Honestly, rock music, in general, has always been in my life, but punk rock specifically... that's a fun story too. They're just a bit long and complicated. I don't normally talk about it too much."

"I'm curious, though. Please?"

Trevor looks in the distance for a moment before looking back at me and smiling.

"Okay, fine. Just because it's you."

Trevor goes on to explain how his mom liked metal and goth music, and because he listened to her CDs after she died he ended up liking that music too from a young age. He says he got into punk rock and that style through a friend named Xida, whose dad owns a punk club in Buschen, the major city near us. It takes me some time to soak it all in. I want to ask about Xida, but would it be rude...? I guess it can't hurt. It doesn't seem like he'd be mad at me for asking, and since I need this conversation to go on, I do it.

"Trevor, can I ask a quick question?"

"Oh, sure, what's up?"

"You keep saying *they*. Is Xida a boy or a girl?"

Trevor looks at me funny before realizing I'm genuinely curious.

"Oh... you know there's more than male and female, right?"

"Like androgynous people?"

"I mean, yeah, but there's more than that. Anyway, Xida's agender. It basically means they don't identify with any gender, whether it be male, female, or anything else outside the binary."

"How does that work?"

Trevor sits his head on his hand for a moment, probably thinking about how to explain it to someone like me.

"Well, it's hard to understand for people who don't have problems with their sex matching their gender, but it's like a disconnect from the abstract idea of gender. Like, being male, female, nonbinary, or anything like that doesn't feel right. Xida doesn't fit into any of those categories. Does that make sense?"

"So Xida is just... Xida?"

"Yeah, yeah, you got it, man," Trevor answers, patting my back. "Also, if you ever meet 'em, Xida uses any pronouns, so don't feel awkward about it."

"I didn't know people could do that."

"It's just how people are."

"Huh, that's cool."

We watch the kickball game for the rest of PE, mainly to watch Emily consistently catch balls without praise. I offer Trevor a tamale before he leaves for lunch. He gets really excited about it, so maybe this whole thing was a good idea. I eat my tamale in a random dead-end hall, hoping Robert doesn't find me.

As I'm eating, I think back on the conversation I just had with Trevor about gender. Of course, I feel like I'm a guy, but to be fair I haven't thought about it before. I know I'm definitely not a girl. I try to think about what it'd be like not to have a gender, but I can't really figure it out. I feel disconnected from myself often, but I don't mind being a guy. Maybe that's because I grew up as one.

I flinch when I hear footsteps approaching, but it's only Andrew. He looks down at me for a long moment, almost like he's examining me.

"You know, Robert skipped after third period to go eat off campus," he starts. "He won't be back. You can sit with us."

Feigning ignorance, I reply, "Oh, cool." Then I remember how to change the subject. "Do you want a tamale? My family made them together over the weekend, and my mom wanted me to give them out."

"Yes, but never mind that right now. You know I saw you this morning. You were walking by as Robert was leaving. Did something happen? He's been acting weird lately, and I still don't know what happened last week at lunch."

Andrew's bluntness is starting to irritate me, and I realize it's the same feeling I had with Robert: anger covering my fear. That's a new concept. Why am I afraid? Andrew seems to know already what's going on.

"Look," I reply, deciding to level with him. "I..."

Suddenly, Robert's words from this morning hit me. If I tell Andrew, he'll know just how weak I am. It will confirm what he's already thinking. I can't show that to someone I barely know at a new school.

"You what?"

"I'll go sit with you all. Thanks for the offer."

"No problem."

We walk back to the table, and as promised, Robert is gone. Finally, the day starts to go normally. I talk with the kids at Andrew's table, I go to theater and listen to Ana and Raina's chatter, I talk to Trevor between classes, and I go home at the end of the day, as it should be.

10

EMILY

___

My mom must be dating someone again. She was gone most of the weekend. Normally, a high schooler with a house to themselves would throw a party or at least enjoy themselves, but I could barely do that. I watched anime and read some books, but honestly, I had felt so disconnected from everything that I spent unknown amounts of time just staring at the ceiling. It still feels weird as I enter school, suddenly aware the bus video from last week is still going around.

Spanish itself isn't bad because Cher, the girl who usually bothers me during this class, minds her business for once, but science with Flanders is annoying. Flanders has a sub today, and he's pretty relaxed in comparison to the usual stuffy teacher we have. He's not yelling at us about how we're writing our lab reports or grumbling about how they used to dissect cats or something when he was growing up. When he has to leave the room for a bit while we continue working on our reports, though, I start to tense up. This won't be good for me.

"Hey, Emily!"

Oh boy. Sanjay. I guess he's going to start it off.

He sits across the room but makes no effort to move toward me or even act like this is a private conversation between him and me. Everyone is staring at us, so I have no choice but to turn around in my seat and address him. He starts asking me stuff about my tomboyishness and whether I'm a lesbian and other BS, and I ask him coldly why he is asking such personal questions.

"Well, you are a man-woman," he replies.

The class releases a synchronous "oooh." It isn't that creative.

I just shrug with a "meh" and go back to work. It's the closest I'll get to being called a guy.

"What? How are you not insulted by that? That's not something you can just say 'meh' to," he continues. Did he really just ask me why I wasn't insulted? He doesn't realize others have called me a he-she species my whole life, which is a far more creative (not to mention hurtful) name.

I turn around in my seat to address him again, realizing I can totally pull a power move. "Dude," I reply. "I get called that all the time. I'm used to it."

"I thought you'd be offended, but I guess I failed," he says.

"No shit, Sanjay."

Everyone goes "oooh" again, and I finally continue working. Now that I think about it, this is my first big incident of the day. Is Robert just lying low?

I almost wish he would stop ignoring me and do something. I don't know if this is worse than him just being direct. At least it was more predictable.

***

Trevor sits down at his usual table by the fantasy section, and I see him with a tamale. I'm glad he managed to get food, but...

"Aren't you... vegetarian?" I ask, my voice sounding hoarse. I overheard him talking about it last year. I quickly gulp, worried Trevor will get mad at me for asking or for knowing personal information like that. Maybe he made a vegetarian one or something. I need to stop being so judgmental.

"You know, Emily," he replies between bites, "the Dalai Lama is vegetarian but will not reject meat if offered to him."

"That's for diplomatic and spiritual reasons, don't give me that," I reply, hoping he gets that I'm teasing. "You can't call yourself a vegetarian and eat meat."

"Well, why aren't you vegetarian, Emily?" Trevor teases, nodding toward my plate with a mystery meat patty on it.

"I can't be."

"And why might that be?"

His question catches me off guard, and then I realize his point. He smirks as I give in.

"Because," I sigh, "like you, I don't have many options."

"Glad we had this chat. This tamale is also homemade by a friend's family, so taking out the meat would ruin the whole thing."

"That's true, I guess."

As lunch quietly goes on, I find myself regretting the whole conversation. What if he took me too seriously? Is it really my place to comment on his food when he rarely brings any? I feel like an asshole. I decide to keep my mouth shut for the rest of lunch. It was probably just my lack of conversation over the weekend that made me talk too much.

The rest of the day is a blur, just like the morning. I was going through the motions. I feel like I'm just a hollow cicada shell. Do other people feel like this? How are others so in tune with reality? Is it because they have no need to escape?

Why do I need to? So many questions to ponder while my legs take me wherever I need to be.

Choir is the only class that got me out of my funk a bit, but being a soprano is proving extremely emasculating. I try to remember that singing is still expression for me, even if it's not low. Besides, the girls have continued the annoying tradition of touching my hair, which I keep telling myself is what they do with guys too. I know they don't see me as one, though. At the concert, I'll have to wear something feminine. I'm already dreading it.

After school, I decide to walk around the outside of the building, away from the back street where Robert was before. It's still hot and humid, especially under my jacket, but the sun makes the colors around me oddly vibrant. This place still must not be real. The colors are all clear and separated, like a children's cartoon. I look down at my hands as I walk, and it's weird to see how messed up my skin is. I don't even notice when I'm picking at my fingers. I must just be dissociating again. I keep looking forward and turn a corner toward the south entrance.

The colors suddenly merge, and my emotions slam back into my body. There's no way he's here. Unfortunately, this now feels very much like reality. I thought I left him behind in middle school—Caston Deng.

He was standing right at the entrance, talking to Corey and Zari as if he didn't mount me in gym class three years ago in front of everyone. I try not to remember, but the memory keeps looping. Him on top of me; noise; the sight and smell of his gross sweat; me trying to push myself out in vain, in vain, in vain; his friends laughing; looking over at the others—the coaches—watching like they couldn't hear my screams of "no!" or "get off me!" It keeps happening. Over and over. I can't scream. He's here. I'm not safe. I need to get out of here, away from him.

They spot me as soon as I turn the corner, and I start running. Running, oddly enough, in the direction of my middle school, across a large, empty field. No matter where I run, I can't truly escape, it seems, as memories of Caston and bullying by his friends fill my brain. Right now, though, I can run somewhere that gets me away from him. I can't let him get me again. As I reach the school grounds, I'm reminded of the forest nearby, on the other side of the school. I know those woods better than they do, no doubt. I finally look back, and luckily I mix in well with the middle school kids leaving for the day, but Corey, Zari, Caston, and now Robert are now all on my tail.

I sprint as fast as I can into the woods, weaving in and out of trees to try to lose them. I have no idea what they plan to do with me. I just know I'm terrified. The same terror I felt with Caston back then. I look around and spot a tree that's easy to climb, quickly working my way up like I often did back in seventh grade. I can see them, and I've lost them for now, but it's only a matter of time until they see me.

"Hey, what are you boys doing in there?"

I see the four of them turn back toward the entrance of the woods, where the voice came from. I can't see who's there, and I'm not sure they can, either.

"None of your business, man!" Robert shouts back to the trees.

"You all are high schoolers. I can call the cops on you for being there, and I will! You know nobody's allowed here. This is private property. You all are trespassing."

The four angrily storm out of the woods, and I sit back against the trunk of the tree, still trying to get my breath back. It's been years, but I can't forget what Caston did. It even seems so minimal compared to what I go through now, but maybe the sexual nature was what made its impact. I didn't know anything about all that when I was twelve. Now I refuse to know anything. Most guys my age are watching porn and masturbating. It's a rite of passage. I can't do either of those without Caston returning to my brain. To have him, Robert, and the twins all rallied against me. It's honestly beyond anything I ever guessed. I managed to get away without a scratch. Climbing these trees in the past really paid off.

After my body finally calms down, I try my best to get down from the tree even though my arms are still a bit numb from panic. I make it down relatively quickly and walk through the woods toward the high school before sneaking out and walking back across the empty field, no boys in sight.

11

EMILY

———

I have no issues on the school bus with physical assaults of any sort. It's just been verbal onslaughts this week from Corey and Zari, with Robert simply grinning behind me. I wish I felt more relieved. Robert's grins scare me, as if to say, "Things can't stay like this forever."

As I head into school and sit on a lonely step in the cafetorium before classes, Jack and some of his friends walk up to me. I get a bad feeling in my stomach. They can't do anything too bad in public, right? Wait, of course they can. Have I learned nothing?

"Hey, I'm here to figure out the truth about you, Emily," he says, trying almost laughably hard to seem serious. I can't help but entertain that.

"Oh, the truth? That I'm some tranny out to destroy your fragile sexuality?" It feels oddly good to use that word for my own benefit, finally. It's been a while since I've even heard it. Everyone just calls me a lesbian now.

"Bitch, you're lying. You don't have a penis."

"I will someday."

"The hell? Fricking freak, come here."

He grabs my wrist and pulls it toward him, forcing me to stand up. He's looking at my gloves. The incident from the math test last week flashes in my head, and I realize what he's looking for. He wants to see under my gloves. I suddenly become conscious of how raw and peeled my fingertips must look, and my confidence from earlier deflates. I stop trying to pull my hand back.

"Ew, what's this? Are you spreading some sort of skin disease? That must be why you wear the gloves, huh?"

"What? No! What are you doing?"

He yanks off my glove with his free hand as I notice one of Jack's friends with his phone pointed toward me.

"Why are you filming this?" I ask, going back to trying to get my naked hand out of his grip. "There's not even anything here, asshole! Look!"

"As a public service announcement," Jack replies for his friend, ignoring his complete failure to find anything he was looking for. "I told you. I'm here to find out the truth. Besides, you're used to videos like this. Aren't you?"

As I'm about to answer, a new voice comes out of nowhere.

"I have a truth for you, Jack."

I let out a small gasp as Jack turns around and whacks Trevor's hand off of his shoulder, growling. "Don't touch me, fag."

"Oh, so you do understand the idea of unwanted touch. I was convinced you'd forgotten, seeing as Emily clearly doesn't want yours."

"Why is it any of your business? I'm trying to answer the question everyone is asking!"

"Oh, who is asking? Please tell me. Besides, isn't it odd you're going out of your way to take off her clothes, even in public? There's a legal name for that, I'm sure. Maybe a few."

"Hey, this isn't the time for your snotty attitude. Let the upperclassmen do their thing, huh? This is America. It's a free country."

"Wow, you're really bringing America into this? Let the hand go."

"No. Why would I listen to you? Juniors know more than sophomores, you know. As someone of higher authority, I need to hold people like you and her accountable."

"If you like America so much, then maybe remember a democracy comes from the consent of the governed. You don't have our consent, so I am going to overthrow you."

"Ha, that's laughable. You can't overthrow me."

"Hmm, you'd make a great fascist leader."

"Maybe I would! What's it to you?"

"Oh, just the fact your friend is recording you saying that and everything else you've said since I arrived. Good luck editing that shit and still revealing your *truth*."

Trevor then hits Jack's hand, and his grip loosens immediately. I'm so bewildered by what Trevor and Jack's argument has turned into that I barely process Jack's group leaving in a huff and Trevor returning my glove.

"Are you okay?" he asks. The question makes me want to cry and makes my heart pound. People don't normally ask that. It's nice to have somebody care. Yet it's embarrassing too, since it's so rare.

"Yeah, I am, just a sore wrist. But why did you do that?" I ask.

"What do you mean? I do this for many people. Assholes are everywhere."

"I never see you doing that."

"I think that's a good thing. Don't you? It's bad to be known for it. I'm not superman or anything like that."

"You just like pointing out people's hypocrisies, huh?"

"It makes them think, doesn't it? Luckily, I saw it all before going to my usual spot. See you at lunch?"

"Oh, yeah. See you then."

Shortly after Trevor leaves, the first bell rings, so I head to class. Amazingly, almost nobody is talking about my incident with Jack and Trevor this morning. Jack's friend must've not been able to edit the footage well enough to post it. That's relieving.

Lunch is awkward for me because I'm still embarrassed Trevor stood up for me, but Trevor seems preoccupied with other things. He's hiding his emotions behind his book, but I get a look at his furrowed brows and glazed-over eyes as he grabs the food I gave to him without even a smirk. I guess now is not the time to talk to him. It's nice not to have to talk about this morning, though.

About halfway through lunch, we both perk up as we hear someone run full speed across the hallway. Even through the closed, thick double doors, we can hear the footsteps. Trevor immediately abandons his book, running after the person. Considering how this morning went, I am slightly scared for the person who seems to have disturbed his reading time. I want to follow, but I should stay out of it. It might end up bad for me.

Lunch ends, and Trevor still hasn't returned. There's no way he'd lecture someone for fifteen minutes over running, right? He's not a stickler for rules. One can only guess with Trevor at this point. He has a small sort of immunity from physical bullying, so maybe that's why he's so confident. Nobody wants to hit the kid with a heart condition. These bullies don't want to murder anyone, just destroy them until they want to murder themselves. That's one way to get away with murder, I suppose. I leave the food behind for Trevor in case he comes back at some point.

Math has a very heavy feel after this morning's incident with Jack. I can feel him jabbing eyes at me whenever my back is turned, something I'm somewhat used to but still bothers me. I try my best to focus on my point-slope form problems, reminding myself not to take Jack seriously. He got what he wanted, and he was humiliated for it. That should keep me safe for a day or two at least.

***

Because yesterday didn't go so well walking outside the school, I decide to walk around the inside of the school while waiting for my mom to pick me up. While walking through the empty halls has its own peacefulness to it, I can't wait until I can drive myself. I'm technically old enough to get a permit, but I haven't even started the process. My mom would be no help, and it probably has forms that ask for information about both parents. Legal forms tend to do that. I always hate those because the "exceptions" are a death certificate or a court order, both of which I do not have.

As I walk past the library, I can hear voices coming out through the closed doors. Wait, that can't be... I peek through the window. It's Robert and Trevor, arguing. I immediately turn and pin myself against the wall next to the doors, hoping neither of them saw me. I can't help but try to listen in, though. If Robert is bullying Trevor, then I have to return the favor and help him, right? Could I even do that?

I think I hear my name. I place my ear near the door, straining to hear more. I can only pick up small bits and pieces, but what I can gather is something about Trevor having photos. I also hear the name Cole, which is odd considering nobody from our grade has that name. Wait, wasn't Cole that freshman from the anime club? The one who sits on the bleachers with Trevor in PE? What does he have to do with this? Why does my name keep coming up too? Is Robert bullying this Cole kid too?

Click.

I try to suppress a scream and jump to the side as Trevor pushes open the library door, bringing me back to reality. He quickly spots me beside him, and we stare in silence. I can still hear Robert shouting profanities of some sort, quieting down as the door closes again. I never realized how much taller Trevor is than me. He's skinny too. Maybe he doesn't get a lot of food.

We both open our mouths to speak at the same time and then close them. We both have big questions for each other that neither of us seem to want to get into. He probably wants to know how much I heard, and I want to know why I was part of their argument. I actually have a lot of questions, but I can't figure out how to ask any of them. We silently decide to walk in opposite directions without asking or answering.

12

COLE

I have the same nightmare again. Normally, it wouldn't bother me, but my mind keeps trying to tell me who is pinning down and hurting me. It has to be Robert, or... It can't possibly be my father, right? He's gone. Not dead, but certainly not around ever. I can't really do anything about it.

Shaking long-rusted memories of my dad out of my head, I eat my breakfast, get dropped off at school, and search around for Trevor. I'm worried about heading to the gym as usual, because Robert might be expecting me. I don't want what happened yesterday to happen again, even though somehow it feels like it was a week ago. I try the cafetorium first, but I see no sign of Trevor. I don't even see Emily, now that I think about it. Not that I know where she'd be in the mornings. Most importantly, though, I don't see Robert.

I decide to take the time to go over my lines for my Hamelin audition, so I sit against a wall and place my backpack beside me. I hadn't processed auditions were in two days, and with family over during the weekend and worrying about Robert, I haven't had time to practice. I read over the script last night, so I at least have a better understanding of the plot than I did before when I skimmed it. This is definitely a watered-down version of the story, but such is the tradition of theater, I guess—a flair for the dramatic to cover the reality of a situation. *Les Misérables* would be boring without music, in my opinion.

When PE comes, I find Trevor in the locker room with his shirt off. I can see a long, discolored scar going down his chest. It looks different from the kind I have from surgeries. Mine are so small, I don't really think about them. It looks old too—the discoloration muted with time. He's about to throw his shirt on but pauses when he sees me staring. I look away, embarrassed.

"It's okay, man," he assures me, his shirt on within a second. "I know it's weird the first time you see it. I normally try to get my shirt on fast, but eh, it's fine. It's from an intense surgery when I was young. Please keep this to yourself." I agree, and we head to the bleachers after changing. Why do we even need to change? I'd rather not have to be in the smelly locker room with screaming and all of that. It's a jungle in there.

While we're watching whatever game everyone is playing, I keep debating whether to tell Trevor about yesterday. I don't know if I can do it. I don't want to compromise his mission. I consider telling him about my nightmare, but I'm scared of what he'd tell me. Hmm, I've been curious about that Xida person and what being agender means. Maybe I can ask about that instead.

"So, Trevor, about that Xida person..."

"Oh, yeah, what's up?"

"Being agender, is that like feeling outside of your body? Like, not really connecting with it?"

"Oh, not at all," Trevor replies. "Agender is just not identifying with the social construct of any gender. It just doesn't *fit* right. It's not an out-of-body experience. Why?"

I feel awkward admitting this, but I know he won't react poorly.

"Well, I feel like that a lot. Like I'm just on autopilot. That's part of why I like watching people and observing. I don't react to things like others do. The concept of a *self* is weird for me. I've noticed it more since coming here. It's like everything is just a stage. I know Shakespeare said 'All the world's a stage,' but it definitely wasn't meant to be literal. I was thinking maybe that all meant I was agender. Like I have the anatomy of a guy, of course, but I don't know."

"Oh, wow," Trevor reacts, his eyes widening. "I didn't know you felt that way. Hmm, how should I put this...?" Trevor replies, thinking for a few moments. "I feel like your experiences with... would you see it as a sort of detachment?"

The word swims around my head, repeatedly knocking into my skull. Detach. Detached. Detachment. I'd never had the words to name it, but yeah, I did feel detached. That's the word.

Trevor scoots forward on the bleacher, awaiting my response.

I nod.

"Okay, well, I'm glad you know," he says. "But your experiences with detachment are separate from your gender. Well, it can be a bit more complicated than that, but for you, it's possible that your detachment is what's known as dissociation."

"Dissociation? It has a name?" I wonder if there's a Spanish equivalent. Maybe it's an official term, though. Trevor seems more serious, so I don't think it's slang.

"I'm not an expert, but what you're describing sounds like dissociation. It's a psychological thing—that autopilot feeling when you don't really connect with the idea of a *self*. Everyone experiences dissociation to a small extent at times, but it's also normally a trauma reaction when severe or in excess. I know people who experience it."

...That took a sharp turn.

"Trauma?" I reply on impulse. "I don't have any trauma, though. My life's been fine, relatively speaking. Moving here is probably the most life-changing thing that's happened. It's probably normal."

For some reason, my nightmare flashes into my head, as does Robert. This is what I was trying to avoid. My palms are getting sweaty now. Come on, Cole, those are not traumas. Don't be ridiculous. Trauma is when people are abused or go to war. This is nothing compared to that.

"Perhaps. Like I said, I'm not an expert," Trevor goes on, looking at my hands tightly gripping the edge of the bench. "But feel free to look into it if it's bothering you. As for your gender, try to think about how you want to be seen in the future. Do you want to be seen as a man? Woman? Something in between? Neither? That can help get your brain thinking about it. I've explored with my gender, and I concluded I'm still a guy. But I know myself much better through that, so there aren't really any cons exploring it. You also get to understand others better."

"Well, I think I want to be a man," I answer.

"It's up to you. Take some time to think about it."

We spend the rest of PE talking about alternative subcultures, as Trevor calls them. There are so many to keep track of, but he mainly focuses on punk and goth stuff. I don't understand it all yet, but it sounds cool. Plus, Trevor is super enthusiastic about it. His eyes have lit up, and he's talking even faster than usual, throwing his hands around as he tries to say everything he's thinking. He slows down when I ask him to, luckily, so I'm able to keep track of what he's saying.

He even takes the time to recommend some Spanish-speaking bands from Mexico and the southern US border. I feel like some sort of apprentice to his knowledge on the subject since meeting him.

Trevor and I part ways at the end of PE for lunch, and I come to regret that. My breath catches as I see Robert in the cafeteria at our usual table, and we lock eyes as I pass. Almost on instinct, I start walking faster, just enough so I don't make a scene and hopefully am left alone. No such luck, though. I end up walking down a dead-end hallway, and he's right behind me. I back up slowly as if he were a bear, which he has the body for. He has a smirk on his face the entire time as I end up backed into an alcove. Damn. Robert knows this school far better than me. Why did I think I could get away?

"Glad we can finally have lunch together today," Robert starts. "What's in that lunchbox of yours today? More tamales? Is that all you ever eat?"

I don't even bother answering, since Robert is already trying to take my backpack. With some muscle and body contortion, he manages to yank it off me. Yesterday flashes through my mind, and I end up pinning myself against the wall to keep balance as I start breathing heavily.

Robert takes out my lunch box and holds up a bag of grapes.

"Wow, is your mom Dolores Huerta or something, Cole? Pick these yourself?"

Okay, now he's really starting to piss me off with the racism. At the same time, I'm surprised he even knows who Dolores Huerta is. This school teaches about worker's rights activists? I know my school in Plano never did. Maybe he only associates her with grapes or something. He probably thinks George Washington Carver is just about peanuts too.

"What is wrong with you, man?" I finally ask, raising my voice. "How are you so racist?"

"Racist?" He laughs. "Man, you can't say anything as a joke anymore, can you? Everyone's so sensitive nowadays."

"No, you're just racist, freaking *gringo*." I don't really know what I'm saying anymore. It's just coming out. I sound angry, but I'm not really feeling it.

"You're calling me racist and then call me a gringo. You need to learn to shut your mouth, or I'll stuff it with my lawn grass!"

Gringo isn't even a racial slur, but I don't dare go into that or everything else messed up about what he just said. It's not even well-thought-out. He can't exactly stuff grass in my mouth right now. Robert's shit is getting annoying.

"Shut up, would you? If you're trying to spite Trevor, he doesn't even know you're doing this! You just hate me because I'm Mexican, and the Trevor thing is just a treat, huh?"

I lock eyes with Robert as he takes a butterfly knife out of his pocket. He holds the folded handle in my direction.

"Don't say another fuckin' word. Let's eat, huh?"

I stay silent, but I'm confused as Robert opens the bag of grapes, taking one out and handing it to me.

"Put it in your mouth."

I do as he says, but I can't bring myself to chew and swallow. I can't do anything but shake in fear.

"What, you're not gonna eat?" asks Robert teasingly. "That's awfully rude."

I gasp when Robert flashes the blade toward me, and the unchewed grape sticks itself right in my throat. Now I'm completely terrified. I can't get it out, and there's no way Robert's just gonna put the knife down and do a Heimlich for me. I try to perform it on myself, but it fails. Robert's just watching me, still smirking. Am I going to die like this? I can't think straight, and I fall to my knees. Robert comes behind me, pushes my head down, and with the same foot kicks me right in the back. I fall to the ground and stay there, finally getting some air. When I look up, I see Robert with the knife still in his hand.

"You better get the fuck out of here."

I grab my stuff and run without thinking. I run all the way to the stairwell on the other side of the school and speed across the second floor to a bathroom, and barricade myself in the handicapped stall. When I finally make it, I find my inhaler and can finally start to breathe normally again. I can't even believe that just happened.

Someone enters the bathroom, and I stay silent again, hoping they don't need the stall or even notice me. I look under the door at the person's shoes, and I instantly know who it is.

"Trevor!"

"Cole? That was you who ran by the library! Are you okay?"

I immediately unlock the door and let Trevor in before locking us both in. Both of us sit across from each other in the stall, and I look away from his face, embarrassed. What do I even say now? Should I even have let him in? He probably thinks I'm weak now.

Trevor notices the inhaler in my hand and asks me what's wrong. The fear I'd been trying to hold in quickly comes out, and I start crying. I tell him everything—everything Robert has done to me lately. Even as I retell it all, I still can't get myself to feel it. Sure, I'm crying and scared, but it feels like somebody else crying in fear. It's honestly weird and sort of annoying. I tell Trevor this too, and at the end he says he's sorry and hugs me. I'm surprised, but his embrace brings me back to myself and feels really comforting.

"I can't believe Robert would do that. I am so sorry you got involved with him. He's a huge racist. I know those girls Ana and Raina from your theater class have had their own arguments with him. Look, this isn't going to happen again. To you or Emily. I mean it."

"How?"

"I know it may be hard now, but just try to trust me. I'll walk you to your classes today and make sure you get home safe. After today, nobody in this school will have to worry about Robert again. I know that won't remove the pain of what he did, though. I'm sorry I didn't notice."

"You did notice. I was just stubborn. I didn't want to tell you because of your plan."

"You should have told me, but at least now I know. Your safety is just as important to me as Emily's. Don't put yourself through that for somebody you barely know. That includes me. Hey, drink some water; your throat probably needs it after something like that."

Trevor tries to get me to drink water and eat some food he got from my backpack, but I'm too scared to do so. Luckily, I can manage a thermos cap of water. As lunch is about to end, Trevor helps me get up and ready for theater and, as promised, walks me all the way there. He leaves with his two-finger wave, and I feel alone again. However, Ana and Raina seem as enthusiastic as ever to see me. Raina's hair is different today. She has a natural afro instead of her usual braids. It suits her very well. She really is good with hair. I consider telling her that, but I don't want her or Ana to get the wrong idea. I end up just asking them about Robert.

"Oh my gosh, Robert, I don't know what's up with him," Raina starts ranting. "It's like his parents are in the KKK or something. He's not, like, an n-word racist, but he is definitely a 'you're-stealing-our-jobs' racist. I think he just likes saying slurs and stuff, which is honestly sick. Why do you ask? Has he said something to you? I'll beat his ass."

"Raina!" Ana warns.

"Ah, no need, no need," I insist. "He just, uh, called me a beaner and said I'd get his lawn grass in my mouth. He also said my mom was Dolores Huerta because I had grapes for lunch."

"Really?" Ana gasps. "That's oddly specific... but horrible! I'm so sorry!"

"You're really gonna tell me Robert is the way he is but knows the names of worker's rights activists?" Raina asks, giggling. "That's rich. He probably thinks George Washington Carver invented peanuts or something!"

"I thought the same thing."

The three of us laugh until the class officially starts, and it's honestly relieving. It feels better to know I'm not alone.

As promised, Trevor walks with me to all my classes, and he makes sure I'm okay before he leaves too. I can tell he feels bad, but I decide not to bring it up. He's being so nice that I think it'd be inappropriate. I didn't realize how scared and upset I still was, so it's reassuring. When we separate at the end of the day, I'm still a little nervous, but I don't feel as alone anymore.

13

TREVOR

———

After school, I make sure Cole is doing okay. Neither he nor
Emily should have to worry anymore after today. I promised
Cole and myself that, and I don't make promises. I just know
promising ensures I'll do my best. Cole is cool and gets my
crass humor and cynicism, so I can make him laugh a bit.
Once he leaves, I head to the library to find Robert. It's an
unlikely place for someone like him, but it's the one place in
school where you can be if you don't have a reason to stay
after school. It's possible he hasn't left yet, and as I pass I see
him inside. He's hiding from faculty.

I enter the double doors, and Robert stares me down.
We're alone. Not even the librarian is here. I know what I'm
going to do though, so it doesn't affect me. I know I'm in the
right. I know I'm fighting injustice. I'm fighting for other's
rights, like my mother.

He asks what I want.

I ask why he choked Cole with a grape and beat him for
no reason. I might as well be direct.

"Well, as if it's any of your business, I needed to go after
someone. I knew it would piss you off if I messed with Cole,
seeing as you have him sucking you off lately. It was funny,

anyway. The first time he seemed so confused. I tricked him good. To think I was gonna be friends with that loser. Today was a blast too. He's surprisingly feisty."

"You can't keep doing this to people," I say. "It's so wrong on so many levels. You could've killed Cole or put him in the hospital, and last week you almost did the same to Emily."

"Ho, boy," laughs Robert. "I told you last week, fag, I have a line somewhere. I'm not a killer. I wasn't gonna kill Cole. I didn't intend for him to choke, and besides, I know the Heimlich. It was fine. You can't scare me with that anymore."

"Man, why do you all think I'm gay?" I ask, purposely faking naivety. "I'm bi, not gay. I can do you *or* your girlfriend. Oh, wait, where'd she go?" Robert growls and clenches his fists, and while it may have been unnecessary, I feel that has been my best response ever to being called that slur.

"Either way," I add, "regardless of whether you say you would kill or not, you're still cutting it close. You can't do that to people. Your rights end where someone else's begin, Robert. You have no right to invade people like that and harm them for your own sick gain."

"I can do what I want to those people!" yells Robert. "They make themselves their own targets! Emoly's so easy. She just goes with it. Cole does too. He's all bark and no bite. You have no business telling me what I can and can't do to them."

"Yes, I do!" I yell back. "They're my friends, and I'm willing to defend them and anyone else you decide to ruin. I won't stand here and do nothing while you do these horrible things to kids who have done nothing to you!"

"Hey, I didn't put the grape in his throat," Robert defends. "I just placed it in his mouth. Cole swallowed it himself. So, technically, he choked himself. I saved his life."

"You know that's not true!" I say, pointing at him, "You used force to get him to swallow it whole. You scared him. You knew that would happen! That's not saving a life. That's being a sadist. You may be an oaf, but you're strategic."

"Why, thank you," replies Robert sarcastically. "I assume you've come with some extra proposal to try to scare me?"

"I have the original picture with me," I warn, holding it up. "The same deal applies, but now to everyone. It didn't even work the first time. You stopped with Emily, but then you moved to Cole, so I fixed it. I also have another thing I can use, since I know just this picture won't cut it for everyone." I don't tell him that I know he has a knife, because I don't want him trying to get rid of it. If I ignore that for now, then after this I can tell admin. He should be suspended, which would be great. I could work out the rest from there.

"Oh yeah?" he challenges. "What?"

"I know how to contact your parents."

"So?" he questions. "It's in the directory. I can get yours or Emoly's or Cole's."

"First off, you can't get mine. Look for it under Kenji. You won't find anything. Secondly, if you were to contact either of their moms, what would you say? Would you call them up and say their kids are liars?"

"No," Robert answers, disgusted. "What would you do, then, if you got ahold of my parents?"

"I'd be honest," I reply. "I'd tell them I'm Trevor Kenji from Robert's class and that I'm concerned about what I see Robert doing to Emily and Cole. I'd tell what I know. I even have photographic evidence, don't I? I'll have pics of Cole too, if necessary. You leave good bruises, you know. How would you like your parents to find out first?"

"Are you crazy?" he whispers. "My parents would kill me."

"Maybe. I wouldn't know," I reply matter-of-factly. "I just know that if you don't want your parents to know, you should stop messing with people. I know you don't just threaten Emily and Cole. They're just your worst-hit targets."

Robert growls but agrees to the terms.

"Remember, if I see anything, this is all going out there. If you feel a need to get out aggression or anger, there are better ways to do it than taking it out on others." As a final note, I add with a smirk, "I recommend therapy, if possible. Now, get away from everyone."

"What do you even know about me, Kenji?" Robert snaps, aggressively pointing at me. "You say I know nothing. Cole calls me a racist, but you all have no idea what the Mexicans have done to my family or me! What all your people are doing to us! My original mom and dad warned me about them. You immigrants and fags come over here to fuck things up!"

He walks even closer to me, but I stay still. I won't let him intimidate me. We stare daggers into each other's eyes as he continues.

"Therapy is some shit for rich people! Not for people like me who had to get shoved around for years whenever their fake parents rejected them, only to end up with shit every time! All it did was confirm there's no way I can be nice to those fuckin' Mexicans. They haven't done shit for me."

Suddenly, it clicks. Robert's a foster child. From what it sounds like, he's just a pawn in the system stuck with a shitty family. His parents wouldn't kill him if they found out about this. They'd send him back. Then he'd really have nothing. Why is he even doing this, then, knowing the consequences?

Mom, what would you do? I ask, turning my gaze away from Robert. I know his past doesn't excuse what he does, but

I also think he's more likely to be hurting himself in some way. No answer becomes clear. I just need to try my best.

"Robert," I breathe, trying to keep my voice calm, "I don't know what your situation is like exactly, but I do know abuse. Hell, everyone you've attacked knows abuse. I'm sorry for what you've been through, but that doesn't mean you can just attack people for who they are. That's Nazi stuff. You're not a Nazi, right? Or at least you don't want to be, I hope."

"Don't play therapist with me, Kenji," Robert warns. "I don't need your games. I speak the truth. I'm not the only one who's been a victim of immigrants coming in and ruining things."

Before Robert's words go too far for me, I give a warning of my own. "Look, of all things to hold on from bio parents, racism is not what you want to keep. Best of luck, but I won't let you use abuse to comb your fragile ego anymore. We're done here."

I turn around and walk out as he swears at me. I open the door and see Emily to my right. Shit. I didn't know she was here. We stare at each other. I wonder how much she heard or how much she's figured out. I can tell she has questions too, but we both know there's not a way to sufficiently explain this. We turn opposite ways and walk off, not saying a word. I feel guilty, but I keep telling myself I did the right thing. I head straight to the front desk. Ms. Brady is still there.

"Can I help you, Trevor?" she asks.

"Yes," I reply. "A sophomore, Robert Kurt, is upstairs in the library, and he has a knife."

"A knife?" she almost yells. "What kind? Is he threatening anyone?"

"He's not now," I reply. "But I know he threatened someone earlier today with it. I don't know what kind. I assume it's just a pocketknife or butterfly or something like that. I'm concerned he might be waiting to hurt somebody."

"Oh my gosh!" she gasps, panicked, and she runs upstairs, calling on her radio for some other person at the school to come up too. Done. Mission complete. I assume I'll have to stay for a bit, but I don't want to. I hope Emily's made it out of the school safely today. The last thing she needs is for Robert to find her.

The admin lady doesn't tell me to stay, and I know my father will not be happy with me coming home late. So, I leave and get home as fast as I can, which is not very fast since I can't run long distances and have to walk. Actually, I might have been able to do some running, but I'm too paranoid. When it comes to my heart, I still get worried. I make tiny sprints when I'm excited, but I don't normally push beyond that because I don't want to be in that damn hospital again. Ever. I've been there too many times.

I don't want my dad to rear his ugly head, but I know what's to come. I brace myself as I enter my porch and unlock the door. Hopefull he hasn't started drinking yet, but I know better by now. My dad staggers into the entryway, and I can see he's buzzed. He screams at me, asking where I've been in slurred Japanese. I don't answer fast enough, and he shoves me into the house and closes the door, so nobody can see or hear what happens next.

I've done the right thing. Whatever he does or says will be worth it. Robert is being stopped. I'm helping to fight injustice. Right, Mom?

14

COLE

Thursday. Audition day. I feel so much better about my audition now that I know Robert's been suspended. Trevor sent me an email about it Tuesday night, but I hadn't really believed him until the school was talking about it all day yesterday. I'm amazed Trevor pulled that off, but he says I helped the most by saying Robert had a weapon. Schools are big on that sort of thing, even back in Plano. I don't want to think about it. Not that I can help that. I have no idea how Emily lasted this way for so long if I'm feeling like this after one week.

Andrew agrees to help me practice lines in the morning before first period, but he's not exactly an actor. He has such a monotonous voice that having him read the other lines feels more like we're studying with flashcards, honestly. I can tell he's trying, though, so I appreciate it nonetheless.

Today, Emily starts sitting with Trevor and me on the bleachers in PE. I'm surprised none of the coaches have said anything, but it seems like they're more focused on the basketball team today. The coaches keep mentioning some upcoming tournament to them, so I'm assuming playing basketball today is a way for the team to get in an extra practice during class.

It's weird, though, talking to Emily now and seeing her up close and interacting with her. Sure, we sat next to each other during anime club, but that was all we did. I really only know about her through Trevor, so I'm a bit uncomfortable. It's just weird, I guess, that she's suddenly just... there. I don't know, but she's nice, at least. Maybe she wants to get to know me better?

She and Trevor talk a lot about music, which I don't really get, but they try to include me anyway. Emily seems to know almost as much as Trevor. Emily also knows about video games, so we get to educate Trevor a bit too. It feels almost normal, especially compared to how weird everything has been up until now. It reminds me of hanging out with Andrew's group before Robert showed who he really was.

Trevor and Emily listen to me practice lines during PE, encouraging me to go for the lead. Emily said even if one of Ms. Castiel's favorites gets the lead role, I might get noticed for a great secondary role. That means I have to learn Hamelin's lines too, but it's honestly a fun distraction.

It just feels so weird that Robert is actually gone—suspended. At lunch, I start to hear rumors that he might even get expelled. The table seems very split on the issue, but I notice Andrew looking over at me the entire time. He doesn't express an opinion, but he was never too friendly with Robert as far as I know. If he knows what Robert did to me, then I probably already know how he feels. I hope Trevor's plan worked. Either way, not having to worry about Robert makes it much easier to practice my lines and ignore lunch conversation as well as Andrew's piercing gaze.

Ms. Castiel put today's theater class as a free period, so people auditioning can practice. Ana and Raina are both trying out for some fun secondary roles, but they keep arguing about whether Ms. Castiel will just typecast them as one of the villager's servants regardless. Looking at the script, I'm almost surprised there are servant roles. These villagers were poor. They made stuff themselves. I guess that's something I haven't had to think about. Nobody said school plays were perfect, and they probably just added the servant roles for the sake of having more roles. Not their greatest idea. I'd hate for Raina to be right in thinking Ms. Castiel would just typecast them like that, but she's been in this town longer than I have. Are people here really like that?

***

When the school day ends, I decide to check by the hallway outside of the theater room to make sure everything is still going as planned. Ana is already there, and it feels weird to see her without Raina. I guess this is my chance to talk to her alone for once. It's surprisingly nerve-racking. I normally don't think too much about what I say, but around her right now, I keep going through different scenarios in my head. What to say, how she'd respond, or if I'll embarrass myself.

When I look back at Ana, I realize I'm dissociating a bit. I guess it's good that I can tell for the first time after talking with Trevor. I'm just watching myself, sitting with this cute girl. She looks further away than she did earlier. Since I don't know what else to do, I start by saying "hi."

"Hey, Cole!" she says excitedly. "Glad you're here! Raina's audition is later, so she isn't here yet, and I need someone to practice my lines with. Do you need help too? We can go back and forth."

"Oh, sure!"

Well, that conversation went way better than expected. We practice until Ana's audition starts, and she sticks behind with me afterward until my turn comes. I've done auditions before, but my nerves still catch up to me as soon as I enter the door to the theater classroom. I didn't realize how much worse it was to be in front of people I didn't know at all. Back in Plano, I at least knew the people in my school's theater department. I take a deep breath to help me embrace my role and act out my lines just as practiced. Ms. Castiel and the other judges seemed impressed at least, but it's hard to tell. Either way, it's now done, and I can leave.

"Oh my gosh, Cole, how did it go?" Ana asks with her great smile. Raina is standing next to her with a similar look of anticipation.

"It went well," I answer, still not totally out of character yet, or am I still dissociating? "Are you going soon, Raina?"

"Yep! Can you and Ana help me prep?"

"Yeah, sure thing."

After about ten minutes, Ana and I are left alone again once Raina's turn comes up. My heart is beating faster next to Ana, and the rest of my body feels warm. I can't think of much to say, so I ask how she is and listen to her talk about her day. She's always talkative, but she keeps up the same energy. I'm sort of jealous she can experience that much emotion.

"Ana!"

Raina's sudden outburst makes both me and Ana flinch as the theater room door closes loudly behind her.

"What parts did they have you read?" Raina asks. "Tell me the truth."

"Oh, well," Ana replies nervously before smiling again, "Castiel wanted me to do that one line from the lady churning butter. I told her I was fine with a smaller role, so she chose that and the nana who yells after the kids. It's fine, though. Really."

Oh no. Those are servant roles. I see Raina's eyes stare daggers at the classroom doors.

"Excuse me a moment, Ana. Cole. I have some business to attend to."

"Raina, no, it's okay! It was probably just a coincidence. She didn't do that to you, right?"

"She was about to until I kept insisting on the role as one of the children. I tried being polite, but she's doing this on purpose. Be right back."

"You won't get the role then, Raina! Castiel won't like you!"

"If she only likes people like you and me in a servant role, then I want her to hate me."

Somebody comes out of the audition room, so Raina takes the chance between auditions to storm in there. The door closes sharply, leaving Ana and me to wonder how Raina is doing in there.

"Man, she always does this..." Ana sighs. "She's right, but she always makes a thing out of it. It's not bad. It just seems so stressful to constantly focus on that. She's darker than me, though, so it might just be more serious for her. I can never tell."

"Is that a bad thing?" I ask. "I mean, this place does seem to have some pretty racist people so far."

"Oh, no, that's not what I mean. It's something I really like about her. I'm not as confident, as you can tell," she laughs. "I'd love to be as strong as her, but we contrast well too. Normally I can talk her down a bit, but I think she expected this and already planned what to do. She's smart like that. Did Castiel do that to you, Cole?"

"No, but I don't really think that's a fair comparison."

"True."

We sit in silence for a bit until Raina emerges from the audition room. We both look over and wait for her to say something as she walks back toward us.

"Man, I'm exhausted... but what's said is said. Ana, do you want a ride home?"

"Sure."

"Cole?"

"You have a car?"

"Yeah, but it's a hand-me-down from my cousin. Nothing great, but it does its job."

"Oh, well, my mom's picking me up, but thanks for the offer."

Ugh, I really want to go home in Raina's car with Ana, but my mom is already on her way. Missed chance.

"No problem. See you later, Cole! Come on, Ana."

Ana also waves goodbye before leaving with Raina, who starts angrily whispering to her, no doubt about what happened just before. It occurs to me once they're gone, I still have no idea what Raina did or said in the audition room. Part of me wishes I could have seen that.

15

EMILY

———

Robert is suspended. Trevor made it happen with Cole, that new freshman from anime club. It's so freaking weird. I'm not sure how to feel about it. I am too nervous about trusting the relief I feel. The idea that Robert might be worse once he gets back honestly makes me angrier than anything else. Trevor explained the whole situation to me yesterday at lunch, but I guess I somehow still feel uneasy about it all. It happened really fast.

However, I did tell myself I'd try to be better friends with Trevor, and I feel bad for Cole, so I end up sitting with them during PE on Thursday. It's honestly been a while since I've had normal conversations with people. It turns out Trevor and I know a lot of the same musical artists, and Cole knows a good amount about video games. Part of me wonders if this is what it's like to have friends. I'd unfortunately forgotten. I've had some friends before, but they all betrayed me in some way during our friendship.

That might be why bad thoughts are still entering my head in this situation. I'm normally used to it when I'm on my own, but it feels weird when I'm actually trying to have fun. Lack of practice makes it harder to fight, but I manage to make it through without Trevor or Cole noticing. I don't need them to worry about me more.

Robert's absence hasn't removed all my enemies, but it's made Corey and Zari harass me less. I can deal with teasing because nobody is touching me. I still have freedom of movement. Jack doesn't even bother me in Algebra, and he's a junior. Honestly, it still just feels like something darker is looming, and I can't shake the feeling. There's still the mystery of whether Caston will be at this school again...

The next anime club meeting is tomorrow, so I discuss some logistics after school with Ms. Simpson and the grade level representatives. All I have to do is make my Japanese language presentation.

It occurs to me while I'm working on it later at home that I could maybe ask Trevor to check over it. I'm way too nervous to ask him for help now, but maybe I can muster the courage in the future as I get closer to him. I'm not sure I should be asking him to do things, though, considering what he's already done for me. Not that I asked for it, either. I don't know how to navigate that. Someone might assume I've figured out social interactions by high school, but that's definitely not the case. It's hard to know the protocol when you're used to everyone trying to trick you. I decide against emailing him for now.

***

The bus ride to school is calm and lonely, as it has been since Robert was suspended. I'm now able to turn on some music with my headphones in and stare out the window. Nobody bothers me, or at least I don't hear any of it.

I find Trevor in the library at the same table where he usually eats lunch, and I force myself to muster the courage to ask him to look over my presentation. I put formal and casual tenses as part of the language lesson, so I want to make sure they're accurate to a native speaker. Just using knowledge from textbooks and anime is not optimal.

"Ne, Trevor," I start, figuring starting with a Japanese intro word would be casual but indicative of what I want. Practice helps anyway.

"Eh? Nani? Ah, I mean, what's up?" he replies, maybe not processing I used Japanese on purpose. So, I ask in Japanese if he can look at my presentation for me with what textbook knowledge I have. I try to remember whether to use ageru, kureru, or morau to ask him to do something for me. It's something that I don't really get the hang of just watching anime. Ageru is giving, I think, so it's gotta be one of the other two. Kureru sounds better, so I pick that one. I think morau is for awards or something like that, anyway.

"Watashi no presentation wo mite kuremasen ka?"

"Un, nan no presentation?"

Oh yeah. I didn't mention what kind of presentation. Of course he'd ask that. At least he replied. If I asked incorrectly, he doesn't bother telling me.

"Ah, anime club no nihongo no presentation da."

"Ah, sou ka."

I plug my USB into the library computer. He asks how I've been learning Japanese, and I mention in English that I do my best to self-study but that it's been limited. He offers to teach me some at some point, and the offer throws me off so bad that I stumble over my words. Luckily, he doesn't seem too bothered and focuses more on the images of anime characters I put in my slides. He doesn't know most of them but likes the art style.

"Ne, do you like visual kei music?" he asks at the end.

"Yeah, but I'm not super into it. It's hard to find bands in the US, but I like the variety in the genre because it's more about the aesthetic."

"Yeah, true. Well, not to seem like an ad, but my best friend Xida is the lead singer for a visual kei band down in Buschen."

"Really?" This piqued my interest. Buschen is a big city, but even big US cities don't tend to have visual kei bands. Not that I would hear about it out here in the suburbs.

"Yeah, they're called Refew if you want to look them up. Xida's voice is amazing. You won't regret it. I'm not in the band, so don't worry, you won't be hearing my voice at all, ha ha."

I return the laugh with a nervous chuckle. "Sounds cool. I might look them up this weekend. It'd be nice to help a small band get running."

"For a visual kei band in Buschen, they're actually pretty popular. They sell out at Xida's dad's club all the time. Haven't you been to the shows in Buschen?"

"I can't really get out much..."

"Oh yeah, no problem. I can't, either—disadvantages of being in a suburb. I go see Refew whenever Xida can drive me, which isn't often, since they live at their dad's club anyway. They're online, though, so you should be able to find them."

Hmm, Trevor seems to be going out of his way to use they and them pronouns for this Xida person. Maybe they're nonbinary? That would mean Trevor might accept me being trans! But what if I'm overthinking it? No, he definitely went out of his way not to use gendered pronouns. I could ask, but I also don't want to ask "Is Xida a boy or a girl?" if they're nonbinary. I guess the worst that can happen with Trevor is that he says no, even if he makes a gross comment or face at me. I don't think that's likely, though, so I decide to go for it.

"Cool, thanks. Also, is Xida... nonbinary? You're only using they-them pronouns."

"Technically, they're agender, but yeah! Normally people don't pick up on that," he replies, his eyes lighting up. "They've been my closest friend since childhood. I think you two would get along if you met, especially since you respect their identity."

Does this mean...? Could I tell Trevor? That I'm... a boy? At just the mere thought of coming out, I can already feel my heart thumping loudly and my hands sweating in my jacket pockets. It reminds me too much of the feeling I had coming out to my mom.

"Are you okay?" Trevor asks, waving his hand in front of my eyes. "You're spacing out on me here."

"Ah, sorry, I..."

I can't do it. I can't say it. Some force starts squeezing my chest, and I can feel my hands start to go numb. I can feel my heartbeat go even faster, the same heartbeat that yearns to come out as male. The heart that was shoved back into the closet two years ago. But... Trevor and my mom are different. I keep telling myself that. This is not the same thing. This is different. Trevor is accepting, and he knows how to keep things private. Maybe my heart is attempting free itself.

"Hey, it's okay, no need to panic," Trevor whispers, slightly bringing me back to reality. "Deep breaths, okay? You're safe in this moment, in the library with just the two of us and the librarian stuck at his computer. Do you need anything?"

I shake my head no to answer his last question. I can't think with my mind fogging up, so I do what Trevor says. Deep breaths. I didn't even realize I was starting to hyperventilate. I look up at the library, which looks larger than it was a bit ago. I hadn't even realized Trevor had moved us behind a library shelf so nobody could see me. *I'm not at home*, I tell myself. *I'm at the library without Robert or anyone else.*

"I'm... a boy..." I sigh, almost involuntarily. I'm too exhausted to try to explain. I barely process that I even said it. I'm just staring at the floor, trying to calm myself down.

"Ah, I see," Trevor says calmly. "I didn't know. Thank you for telling me, man. That looks like it was hard for you to do, but just know I believe all trans people are valid. Including you."

An odd mixture of disbelief and relief flows through me, confusing my brain, no doubt. I've never heard that before. I am valid—as I am. Not some waste of space and resources. Not a faker or a lunatic. Not all those things I've heard from my mom. I make eye contact with Trevor, and he gives me a thumbs-up. My stomach sinks.

"Fuck... Trevor, why?" I ask. "Why are you saying that?"

"What do you mean?"

"I thought you'd tell me I was faking it. Or give me some speech about how I'm just a confused lesbian or something. That's what other people have done. Why can't you just say the same thing?"

Trevor pauses for a moment. He must be thinking about how pathetic I'm acting. How I don't even have the spine to take a compliment or even just acknowledgment of who I really am. How, like everyone else, I'm really just a freak to him on the inside.

"Look, man, I haven't been through what you have, but I've known Xida my whole life. I've watched them go through coming out, harassment, research, the turmoil of dysphoria, and even just how much it hurts them to be constantly misgendered. Speaking of which, do you want me to use male pronouns for you when we're in private?"

I nod. That sounds great. All I can muster verbally is a "thank you" before my throat catches on my breath and my eyes get watery. That counts as crying for me. That's the most my eyes have watered in a while. My breathing and heart rate finally settle down as my tears beg to be freed from my eyes.

"How long has it been?" I ask.

"I'm not sure, actually. Let's check."

We both walk out from behind the shelf and look up at the clock. The first-period bell is about to ring. We head back to the computers, and I make sure I have everything saved and in my backpack. Trevor has nothing on him. He must be using his locker. I can't do that. I get too paranoid about someone stealing my stuff. The locks are notoriously broken here. We uneventfully go our separate ways just as the bell rings.

16

COLE

___

I know the audition results won't be released until Monday, but I pass by the theater room in the morning before first period anyway. You never know. When I go to the gym, I find Andrew and everyone as usual. Andrew perks his head up as he notices me, but he quickly looks away. The awkwardness is too much for me, so I sit slightly away from the group. I feel bad. I haven't told Andrew what's happened, and he's shown concern. I feel a need to apologize, but I also don't know him well yet.

To my surprise, Andrew breaks from the group and sits next to me. Normally, Andrew doesn't show much emotion on his face, but he looks... nervous. He keeps looking at me and then away, tapping his toes on the gym floor.

"I'm sorry," I say, barely looking at him. I guess this means I'm nervous too.

"You know what?" He sighs, closing his eyes. "It's fine; it's not like you owe me anything. I don't blame you. At least Robert's gone for now. Nobody else is bothering you, right?"

"Yeah, luckily."

We awkwardly sit until the five-minute bell rings, and we go our separate ways. Nothing of note happens in my morning classes except for Ms. Rowan prompting me again about her proposal that I write more, or at least get more in touch with my emotions. I have been writing journal entries since my first incident with Robert, but I don't tell her that.

In PE, Emily participates in the game today since it's kickball again, so it's just Trevor and me on the bleachers like it was last week. That's fine, though. I'll see Emily at anime club. I want to talk to Trevor alone, anyway. In the silence, the only thing I can think about is that nightmare.

I've been trying to ignore it, but it's happening almost every night in some form. The same person is pinning me down, not knowing where I'm feeling pain, and my mind trying to make it someone who it can't be. I don't even remember my dad. How can the dream be about him? It must be about Robert. I guess if it is about Robert, then I should let Trevor know. I tell him about the nightmare, Andrew, and the fact that I think I should be more freaked out about it all. He brings up dissociation again, but I admit I haven't looked into it yet.

"What about Wednesday?" he asks. "Do you remember the knife incident as clearly?"

I think about it. I guess not. Now, it seems all a blur. I can describe exactly what happened, but I can't visualize it in my brain. It makes me question some stuff, but that's always what happens. Good thing I wrote it down last night. I can fact-check myself.

"No," I admit. "It's all sort of muddled now, although I could tell you what he did. I just wouldn't be able to truly remember it. In a bit, it'll probably become a fabricated memory. Once it gets to that point, I can explain, but I won't know if I'm telling the truth. That's why I'm trying to understand emotions better."

"Weird," says Trevor, fascinated. "So, for you, does forgetting the memories mean you don't feel their impact?"

"Kinda," I reply, unsure. "Everyone back in Plano said they were surprised I was so calm and happy. I can see where they get it from too. I mean, I have lung issues, and I don't have a dad. Now I've just moved to a new town, not to mention all the social stuff in between. Just going with the wind is a good way to explain it, I guess."

"So, you don't remember your dad?"

"Nope." I then look at Trevor, trying to read him, but his body language doesn't give anything anyway. Is he implying that my dad did something really bad?

"Oh, sorry," he apologizes. "I just got curious. I don't know what it's like not to have a dad."

"No, it's okay," I tell him. "I just know what my mom told me. He left when I was five. She's never told me why other than there were a lot of issues. I mean, I'm used to it just being my mom. It's all I know. So, it doesn't really bother me. Besides, my mom's not too bad."

"Oh, wow, I lost my mom when I was also five. That's a spooky coincidence. I don't remember much, but I know the stories, read the internet articles, and all that. It kind of helps me fill in the blanks pretty well."

"Oh, I'm sorry."

"It's not a problem. Guess we're more alike than I thought."

Relieved to hear that, we then talk about music, and once again I listen as Trevor enthusiastically relays the history of all these obscure bands. It's like I really have a friend. Sure, we're only talking about something he knows, but it doesn't bother me. I finally have a friend.

Theater goes well, especially with Raina and Ana giving off their usual energy. Ms. Castiel seems unfazed if Raina said anything especially bad yesterday during the auditions. It's tempting to ask, but I don't want to make Raina angry by having her relive it again.

While leaving theater class to go to my next period, Trevor is standing against the other side of the wall. He hasn't done that since the incident with Robert, but it's a relief to see regardless.

"What's up?" I ask.

"Yeah, are you free tomorrow?"

"Maybe. I'm not sure how much I have to do with my family this weekend yet. Why?"

"Well, I thought we could hang at the park. Xida will be there too, and you both can meet each other. Oh, shit, you probably don't know which park I'm talking about."

"I don't, but I'd be willing to go if my mom will drive me."

"Right on, right on. Just have your mom drive you to Grandeer Park tomorrow. Does around noon work for you?"

"It probably will. I'll text my mom and ask. Is it something with Xida's band?"

"You'll see."

"Um, okay then."

I send my mom a text as Trevor and I walk to our next classes. Maybe Trevor is just setting up Xida and me to meet so we can be friends. Trevor hasn't really seen me with people besides him, now that I think of it. He knows about Andrew, and Emily is starting to hang with us now. However, it's not like I'm super close to either of them. Well, I want to meet this agender person anyway. It'd be interesting to see how they think.

After school, Andrew approaches me before I go to anime club. He warns me that Robert is coming back so the school can talk to his parents. That means I have to lie low. I tell him I have anime club, and he seems relieved, heading out right after. I guess he has been worried about me. Maybe I have more than one friend now. Heeding Andrew's warning, I get to the anime club room as fast as I can. Emily still hasn't arrived by the time club's started, and I get a bad feeling about that.

Ms. Simpson eventually asks someone if they know where she might be, and although I don't know, I find myself volunteering to find her. As I walk out into the hallway, the walls seem to sway, and I suddenly realize I don't really know where I'm going at all. I try to listen for sounds, but it's hard to make out anything with all the buzzing of electricity and air conditioning.

I think I hear something downstairs, so I quietly head down a nearby stairwell and try to listen again. I hear an echoing sound from the direction of the music hall, and as I quickly walk over, I remember that as the place where Robert attacked me. Only random string and brass notes can be heard. Turns out it's only band practice.

I still have a bad feeling in my stomach, so I head across the school and suddenly hear a thud above me, jolting me back to reality again. I run back upstairs, and then I see red. Vivid red.

17

EMILY

———

After school, I know I have anime club, but I decided to walk around a bit before it officially starts. I'm not sure it calms me down today, however. I'm thinking too much.

I keep my head down and my hands in my pockets. I pass by a few people, who thankfully don't bother me, although I flinch each time. Is this who I have become? Somebody who is hesitant of everyone, even himself?

I keep walking until a figure appears in front of me, startling me, putting his hand on the nearby locker and leaning against it. I snap my head up, and Robert looks down on me with a little gleam in his eye. I can feel the color leaving my face in terror. What is he doing here? He's supposed to be gone. This is why I'm so anxious around people—him.

"Hey, Emoly. I've missed you," he chides. "Want to have some fun?"

I try to turn around and run away, but Corey and Zari have suddenly appeared behind me. I'm surrounded. My heart starts pounding as I realize no teachers are nearby.

"Why are you even here, Robert? You're supposed to be gone!" I yell, trying to stop my voice from quivering.

"Oh, shush. I'll be gone soon enough, after the school finishes talking to my parents," Robert replies. "But I need to finish off with a bang, you know? It's no fun just going from school to school with nothing to be remembered for. I'm taking this as a 'fuck you' to Trevor. No admin will be able to see this, being too busy with my folks."

I look over at Corey and Zari, who must have known about this, and they start laughing.

"You thought we'd just leave you alone forever?" Corey asks.

"A false sense of security is much better," finishes Zari.

"And the admin didn't bother to keep you in the office?" I was floored. Why would they let him just wander?

"You think they care? I was told to just not cause trouble. It's not causing trouble if I'm doing the same stuff I normally do with you, right? Besides, if anyone discovers us, I'm already gone. You have to live with it. Remember it. Remember me."

Corey and Zari both pin an arm behind me using my hoodie sleeves, and a jolt of panic finally unleashes itself. Since when is Robert this forward-thinking? This cunning? I've always seen him as just doing whatever came to mind in the moment... What could he possibly do with more time to plan?

Corey and Zari pull down on my arms, making me fall on my butt. I manage to pull my legs to my side while trying to get up, but I can't do much else. Honestly, I'm not sure I want to fight it at this point. I should have known this was all too good to be true. One person alone can't stop this madness. I should have never trusted anyone to save me. I guess I'm just too obsessed with the fantasy.

Robert walks behind me, switching grip on my right arm with Corey, who walks in front of me with an undeniably evil grin.

"Why did you all switch?" I ask.

"Oh, Zari and I are letting Robert have his fun now. We're just here to keep you in line."

I glare up at him, and he keeps eye contact with me for what seems like forever. Just staring each other down.

I gasp as a sharp pain sears my forearm.

No way.

Robert's cutting my arm... with a knife.

"How would Trevor feel knowing he did this to you, huh?" Robert asks from behind me. "Thinking he's so great, but look at you, cut up like a little attention whore. He'll regret ever fucking with me or even caring about you, if he ever even did."

I am so terrified I can't even reply. I can't scream. People talk about fight or flight instinct, but I am definitely just frozen. I feel like I can only hear my breath and my heart, both getting increasingly intense. My forearm hurts badly from the cut, but my body is starting to feel cold and hot so rapidly that I can't tell if the coldness on my arm is blood.

It happens again.

I can barely register if he does it anymore since I am in a full state of panic. I still can't move. I can see my vision tunneling, and I can't stop my heart from trying to escape through my throat.

Suddenly, I hear a voice in the distance, and my arms drop limply to my sides as I hear Robert, Corey, and Zari run away. I still can't move much, but my breathing soon starts calming down. The sudden release of tension makes me extremely tired, and I fall onto my side in the middle of the hallway.

18

COLE

———

"Emily... estás bien?" I ask, slowly approaching. I'm still breathing heavily from the moment before. It occurs to me I have no idea how much Spanish Emily knows. It was just a force of habit. She doesn't answer right away, so I nudge her shoulder, trying not to freak out about the blood oozing onto the tile.

Emily turns her head to look at me and asks breathily, "Cole? What are you doing here? How did you get rid of them?"

"I yelled like a teacher from around the corner, and they ran off," I explain. "I'm honestly surprised it worked. Anyway, can you stand? We should take care of your arms."

"I can try, but I am exhausted," she says. "When he started to cut me, I—I had a panic attack. I'm not sure I can stand up. It's okay. I deserve this. You can leave me here."

"No, I'm not going to do that," I answer. "Not after all this..."

"That's... true. I'm sorry about that."

"Don't be. You're on the ground right now. Here, I'll carry you to a bathroom so I can make sure you're okay. Bueno?"

"Sí, sí, whatever you want."

I try helping Emily up, but she isn't very stable on her feet. I soon decide to carry her to the nearby men's bathroom, making sure she doesn't fall asleep. When I put her down on the floor of the stall, I finally notice the slices on her hoodie sleeves. Robert just cut through them. I hope that means the wounds won't be as bad, and that must have been why there isn't a trail of blood. The sleeves absorbed it all. I look down at my own arms, covered in blood, similar to sweat. Well, as my family would put it, *necesito sudar sangre* para Emily. Blood, sweat, and tears. I need to make this right.

When she can finally sit up decently, I pull up Emily's sleeves and see raw, red stripes on each forearm. I try to put one hand's worth of pressure on each arm with some paper towels, and the bleeding finally stops after a minute or two. It could have been worse. He could have gone for the wrists or something like that.

Emily stays quiet the entire time while I work on her arms and clean off her sleeves in the sink. As I'm doing so, a wave of guilt washes over me.

"I'm sorry," I say.

"What? Why?"

"This isn't right."

Emily has no reply, so I keep scrubbing the sleeves with soap and cold water. I try to get as much out as possible, even though the blood does not show up much on the black hoodie. While doing that, I can't really think about anything else. Just scrubbing. Scrub out Robert. Scrub out that nightmare. Scrub out whatever dissociation is. Scrub out everything unreal and wrong. Scrub out the *mala sangre*. Scrub it all out. What even is this place? How does something like this even happen?

"Cole! It's okay. It's all done."

Emily positions her head within my field of vision, trying to make eye contact. I immediately snap back to reality, let go of the sleeves, and apologize. I'm not sure what came over me, but Emily doesn't ask any questions about that. Instead, she asks about anime club, which I'd almost forgotten about.

"Do you really want to just go back after this?" I ask. "I can tell Ms. Simpson I couldn't find you."

"No, no," she says. "I have to give the Japanese lesson and all that."

"You were literally just attacked. You're still faint. Shouldn't I get you to the nurse at least?"

She vehemently shakes her head.

"Cole, I know we don't really know each other, but sometimes, acting like nothing happened is good. If I can go back upstairs, give the presentation, watch anime, and clean up after, it will feel less like something went wrong."

"But... you're still bleeding, and your jacket's covered in blood. It's black, but I can still see it. I'm not even sure I treated your arms properly. What if they get infected? You can't just go back. Should we wait a bit longer, at least? Or, as I said before, I can tell Ms. Simpson I couldn't find you."

She sits for a minute before responding.

"I guess... I can just wait here and leave after club lets out. My mom tends to be a bit late anyway."

"I guess that works. Do you want me to stick around, though? I want to make sure you're okay."

"I'll be fine. Just leave me alone."

By the time club is over and I check on her again, she's gone.

***

At around noon on Saturday, my mom drops me off at Grandeer Park, and she immediately takes a liking to Trevor, who has his mohawk up for once, when she sees a patch of some Mexican band she likes attached to Trevor's jacket. This surprises both me and Trevor. I never knew my mom listened to rock music. I figured my mom was the type to tell me Trevor was a delinquent, but it seems I don't have to worry about that now.

We silently walk past the park down some paved path into a more wooded area. The concrete ends and turns into a beaten dirt trail. When we finally make it through the trees, I see where this is going. We're at a graveyard. I'd never been so close to one, and it gives me a bad feeling.

"I need you for this, Cole," he says, reading my worries. "Please. You don't have to come in with me if it's too much, but I really want you here." I look at the graveyard again, gulp, and let Trevor take me in. I want to support him. I'm certain I know who's in here. I resist the urge to read the gravestones and focus on Trevor's back as we walk to a grave in the corner that seems well-kept, where some-one with bright blue hair is sitting in front of a bouquet of white flowers. This must be Xida. They're entirely covered in bulky clothing with a bandana over their face, so I can only see eyes and hair. I can't tell their gender at all, but I guess that's the point if they're agender. They seem about our age, if not a bit older.

Xida waves at me and hugs Trevor. I don't really know what to say, but luckily Trevor introduces us. I shake Xida's hand and notice the top part of it feel very rough. I look down out of curiosity, but I look away once I realize it's scar tissue. I don't say anything about it as Trevor joins Xida on his knees, and I follow suit. Xida burns an incense that they say is culturally significant to the Japanese, but they don't explain any further.

The gravestone seems to be made of marble and has a fancier Gothic font compared to the other nearby graves. It reads, "Here lies Kairi Cecilia Kenji. Beloved wife of Morido Kenji, daughter of Rika Kaori and Hayao Kaori, mother of Trevor Kenji, and philanthropist. May 6, 1972–September 5, 2004." September 5? That's today. Now I know why we're here. I remember Trevor saying she died when he was five. That's really sad. It's been just over a decade. To think he still comes... but I guess I would do the same.

There's also a quote below the dates that reads: "People don't always live to be happy; they live to be satisfied. Everyone has a right to reach their personal level of satisfaction."

It's a beautiful quote. "She said that at one of her speeches, originally," Trevor tells me, breaking the silence. "But she always said it to me too, to tell me how everyone deserves fair treatment. My dad had let me choose that quote even though I was only five, because I wanted so badly for her grave not to be lost. I don't know if it was her most important quote, but I know it should be here. It reminds me of all she fought to improve the lives of everyone in Buschen—all I need to fight for." He and Xida stroke the stone almost nostalgically.

"Kairi was more than a philanthropist to me. She was essentially a mother to me as well," Xida finally says. "She practically raised us together. This is a mother I can still visit."

That statement was pretty ominous, but I decide it's best not to ask for clarification. Trevor starts talking to the gravestone.

"Hey, mom," he starts. "I'm here again, and this time with Xida and my friend Cole. Cole and I managed to take down a school bully, although it hasn't been easy. What Robert is doing is something I know you wouldn't tolerate."

I flinch impulsively. Trevor is saying that, but he has no idea what happened to Emily yesterday. Guilt stirs in my stomach, but now is not the time to tell him. I push out memories of Emily's bloody arms, her face... no, I need to focus on Trevor right now. He's talking to his mom.

"If only I could have been as strong as you to do something sooner or think it through better. I am fighting, though, in my school and everywhere else, so I can continue your work. Even in Buschen, people still remember you too. They still are grateful for what you did for them and the city. Dad's the same as he was, though... sorry he couldn't be here. I'm sure he's only the way he is because he misses you even more than I do. I love you, Mom. Every day I wish you were still here to see me."

After that, Xida starts in, but Xida speaks in Japanese. I guess Trevor must have said his words in English so I would understand. It feels weird that he talks about all that Robert has done, but he still doesn't know about what happened to Emily yesterday. After Xida is done, I ask what happened to Trevor's mom. I'm not sure if it's an appropriate question or not, so I tell Trevor he doesn't have to answer.

"No, it's fine," he assures me. "I wanted to tell you today anyway. Xida's here for emotional support, so I'll be fine."

Xida nods and puts their arm around Trevor's shoulder. "Yeah, I got him."

Xida's voice is higher than I expected, but oddly enough, I still can't determine their gender. They really must be genderless.

"Well, as you know, I was five when it happened. I don't remember much, but I know the story well enough. I was about to have major surgery on my heart, and the survival rating wasn't super high. My mom had to take care of some stuff back home, but she promised to be back before my surgery. However, they had pushed my operation up an hour, and my mom had to hurry to get to the hospital on time since it was such short notice. I do remember I was scared shitless. I understood I might die, and I wanted to see my mom again. I wanted her to be there for me, because I knew she'd make it all better. My dad tried to reassure me she'd be there afterward, but it didn't help. I even tried to refuse the surgery until she got there, which obviously didn't work. I went in anyway."

Trevor looks over at Xida as the wind picks up, and I can feel the friendship—or chemistry—between them. I've never seen two people look at each other so lovingly. Could Xida be...? No, Xida is basically like a sibling to Trevor, right? Since his mom took care of them both? Maybe it's just a strong brotherhood thing... either way, I can't help staring. Trevor nods silently, and Xida rests their head on Trevor's shoulder, facing me. Then Trevor continues.

"After I woke up, I realized I was alive. My dad wasn't there, though. The doctors told me he had business to take care of. They kept me until they knew I was in stable condition, and then they had my dad come in. I asked him where Mom was, and that's when he told me that Mom had died in a car accident on the way to the hospital."

I'm in shock now. I don't know what to say or even if I should say anything yet. Trevor takes a moment to excuse himself and look over at Xida's head, still on his shoulders but with their eyes closed.

"Are... you... they... um, are you all okay?" I finally ask. Trevor and Xida both nod, although Xida seems a bit fidgety. Trevor insists he's fine and briefly checks on Xida before continuing. I imagine hearing this is hard for Xida too.

"I didn't say anything at the time. I knew what death was. They had a therapist come see me, but they couldn't get me to talk. It resulted in me staying in the hospital longer since the event put stress on my heart. I found out a few years later she was T-boned by a drunk driver and that her actual cause of death was cardiac arrest from the shock of the crash. If she'd had a healthy heart, she'd still be here. She never knew if I survived the surgery or not. I want her to know I survived. I don't want her to think I'm dead and that it was all for nothing.

"On the day of her funeral, the doctors let me go because my therapist insisted it would do me well. My dad had invited about a hundred people but also had it open to the public. It was on the news and everything, but of course, he hid that from me. You know how many people showed up to the funeral, Cole?"

I'm scared to answer, and I bet it's rhetorical anyway. Xida's smile suggests good news, though.

"Thousands. Literally, over five thousand people showed up. It made me feel a bit better that so many came. They were all kinds of people, seemingly of all backgrounds. Some individuals, some were in large groups. They'd all come to pay their respects. My mother had done something for all those people. Even minor things, people said, made a huge difference to them. A lot of them even came up to my father and me, telling us how sorry they were and what an effect she'd had on them. It was sad, of course. I couldn't even talk to anyone, but it was also so inspiring. My mom had been a local hero. My mom was loved by so many. I wish I remembered it better. It was beautiful, but..." He takes a deep breath and looks up at the sky before continuing. "I still thought I'd killed my mom."

"What?" I say without thinking. "How?"

"I've always thought I was responsible for her death, but I'm better about that now. I do like the theory that her heart transferred to mine."

Holy shit—what a huge load to bear.

"What about your dad?" I ask. "Why isn't he here too?"

"He's... had a lot of drinks," Trevor answers. "He's done this the past few anniversaries. That's why I always make sure to mention him to Mom. Even if he doesn't come, I know she'd still want to know about him."

I just nod because I have no idea how to respond to that. It seems normal to him, so maybe reassurance is not the best move.

Much to my relief, Xida asks Trevor if he wants to go back to the park for lunch. The two of them seem to have already picked out a place that delivers for me to try out. It's a Japanese restaurant they claim is the most authentic from the city. I'm surprised a restaurant in Buschen would deliver all the way out to a suburb like Rosedale, but maybe they're closer than I think. I don't know what to get, and after listening to Trevor and Xida rave about all the choices, I pick some miso soup, fried tofu, and some sashimi.

While we wait, Trevor and Xida take no time at all to start playing on the playground. Xida runs around the playground structure, chasing Trevor through steps, bridges, and monkey bars until they both throw themselves haphazardly down the slide at the end, laughing and making jabs at each other the whole time. The way they enjoy themselves compared to how somber the grave visit was is an amazing contrast, but I guess it's good they're able to live their lives despite what happened.

19

EMILY

Saturday morning comes with the soft chirps of birds and no other sounds. No TV, no microwave beeping, no papers were shuffling around, no typing. I look over at my clock. Maybe it's too early for my mom to be up.

It's 10:00 a.m.

My mom isn't at home.

Guess that means I have the house to myself for now, at least. I can eat breakfast and watch anime out loud. I have to be careful, though, because I have no idea when she's coming back. I also know I have to clean the house while I'm here, or she gets mad. She somehow always expects to return to a spotless house when she's been gone for the day.

I walk by her laptop to see if it shows why she hasn't returned, and I see a window open for a dating site. I look closer, and it's her profile.

My mom's with some man-slut. I don't even know if it's the same one as before. If she's staying overnight with this man, then I don't have to be told what that means. She probably won't even tell him she has a child. Perhaps she won't need to, because they'll have another.

I catch myself jumping to conclusions, so I try to think about this objectively. Mom's out overnight with a man, not necessarily a man-whore, for the first time. They may sleep together, but they probably won't have *real* sex. I'm just angry about her dating someone.

When my mom returns at eight in the morning on Sunday, I know better than to say anything, especially since she has a special visitor. I know what to do. If he sees me, mom will be pissed. I tiptoe as quietly as possible into my bedroom and quietly shut the door. It's not like she's done this too often before, but I know I don't exist to her. It's implied at this point. I, ironically, head into my closet, so I know that no light from my laptop will peek out, and the closet will muffle any accidental sounds. I try to just relax and watch something or play a video game, but I can't help but eavesdrop.

"Wow, what a nice house," I hear him say as they enter. "I'm surprised you live here all on your own."

Yep. I made the right decision to hide in my room. Neither of them knows I exist. Maybe I don't.

"Yes, I do," my mom says, cheerier than I've ever heard her. "It's hard to maintain all by myself."

Well, good thing I cleaned up yesterday, bitch.

They tour the house together, and when she reaches my room, she says she used to have a child that died of pneumonia a bit over a year ago.

Pneumonia? I have had it before, but it was years ago and only lasted a week. She's been neglecting me for longer. I guess that's the only half-truth she can find about me.

"Wow, I'm so sorry. Do you use these rooms to help keep her memory?" the man asks.

"Well, yes," my mom answers in her fake-pity voice. "But it's so painful to think of right now. I don't normally open the doors. I want to keep everything just how it was before. Before my beautiful child left me."

Now, doesn't she deserve to be called a bitch? Killing me off for the sake of some man she just met in real life. I know I mean nothing to her, but this is worse.

Since basically all the upstairs has my rooms, including my small game room, my bedroom, and my bathroom, she explains that she wants to keep things as they were when I was alive. He says it'll all be okay because they'll use the stuff for their baby. I hope they're not serious.

She laughs, her high-pitched sound from hell echoing off the hardwood floors.

I start to cry silently, throwing my face into my knees to absorb my tears. I bite my sleeve to prevent myself from throwing my fists against the wall in anger. Whatever baby they have, let's hope they treat it far better than me. Having it be born to different parents entirely would be a good start, though. Maybe I'm jumping to conclusions again, but I can't tell anymore.

They head back downstairs, and the man says he's sorry about the child. Bile comes up into my mouth. He's about to leave, but then my mom insists they do something else together since she's a lonely, empty nester. He agrees, and they both leave to see a movie. They're just gonna make out the whole time, though.

Once they leave, I slowly crawl out of my closet while stretching out my legs, barely able to feel my tears going down my face. I don't even know if they're flowing or just stuck.

I'm not dead, but I wish I were right now.

Or maybe I am a ghost. I couldn't be dead, could I?

I head to my bathroom and look in the mirror. There is only one reflection, so it must be mine. I pick up the toothbrush I haven't used in a while and throw it at the mirror. It comes back to me and hits my shoulder. So, I do exist. I'm not a ghost. I'm alive. That gives me less joy than one might expect.

I touch my fingers on the mirror and realize my hand and the reflection's hand don't quite touch. Even another world is out of reach. I have to stay in this one.

Wait.

I have to be here, but nobody said I have to be *here*...

20

EMILY

I search for Trevor in the morning at school, but he is not in the library like he usually is. I speed-walk through the second floor to no avail, but the large crowd loudly scrambling to get a glimpse of a poster across from the theater room on my way back down the winding stairs reminds me the audition results are up. Maybe Trevor's there with Cole, although then I wouldn't be able to ask Trevor about what I want to do. Even if they're not there, it'd be nice to know if Cole got a good part. I push through the crowd, trying to ignore the echoes of shouts, lockers, and shoes on the tile floor, until I finally see the red hair that signals Trevor. I wonder what his mohawk looks like when it's up. He probably can't put it up in school.

Cole is, of course, with Trevor, and they seem excited as I continue to squeeze my way over. There must be at least fifty people gathered here, either trying to see the poster or trying to get to class through the crowd. Once I finally reach them, I ask Cole how he did while trying to find his name in gold font on the magenta poster.

Suddenly, memories of last Friday come into my head. I must have been so preoccupied with my mom's situation and finding Trevor this morning that it overshadowed last

Friday's events for a bit. Now I'm nervous about how cheery I sounded, but maybe he'll see it as a good thing. I'm self-conscious about my cuts even though I made sure my jacket covered them, and I don't want to be stuck in this crowd now if Robert could be around. Is he finally gone? What will people say if they notice?

"Hey, Emily!" Trevor yells above the clamor of voices, scaring the shit out of me for a split second. "Did you hear? Robert's been expelled!"

"Wait, for real?"

"Yeah!" Cole adds, "You know we wouldn't joke about that."

Oh. Right. Trevor doesn't know about last week, but Cole does. He wouldn't lie to me, right? It feels like a weight's been lifted.

I finally look closely at the audition poster. The leads are who I expected, since Ms. Castiel likes putting her favorites in those roles, but I see Cole's name next to the part for town mayor. For a freshman, that's a big deal. It's the part he was originally trying out for anyway before Trevor encouraged him to go for the lead. So, Trevor's plan worked out again. Does Trevor read minds or something? Maybe he's just lucky.

I congratulate Cole and tell Trevor I'll talk to him at lunch before squeezing my way out of the crowd and heading across the hall to Spanish, their echoes following behind me.

When lunch finally arrives, I give Trevor some extra snacks I got with my lunch and sit next to him at the table in the library. He isn't reading a book, and he seems fully prepared to talk to me, which honestly makes me more nervous. I worry about the librarian too, but he is constantly on his computer. I doubt he'd listen or care if he overheard, but this is also a very serious issue. I make sure Trevor knows we both need to be very quiet about today's conversation.

"So, before you start," Trevor says, "Cole told me about what happened with Robert on Friday. I... I'm really sorry that happened. I have no idea why the school let him just go do his own thing. He's not the planning type, either. I don't know what else to say. Just know he's actually gone now."

"I see..." I guess he did know this morning. That must've been why he made sure to tell me. My scabs start to hurt as I think about it. I soon shove it out of my head and go to ask my question. He must relate. His situation doesn't sound too great either, from what I've heard.

"Hey, Trevor?"

"Yeah?"

I look briefly toward the librarian's office and back before whispering, "Have you ever thought about running away? Just in general."

"What the actual hell?"

I shut up immediately. Did I offend him? Am I crazy for thinking this? Is he going to tell me how ungrateful I am? Well, he can't be too mad if he was still able to keep his voice down, right?

"Oh no, shit, don't get nervous," he explains. "I mean that because after this weekend, I've put serious thought into doing that. Running away, I mean. You remember Xida?"

"Your friend with that band?"

"Yeah. They can take me in."

"Wow... I don't even know where I'd go. I haven't thought that far. I just need to get away from my house. It's better off that way."

"How serious are you about it?" he asks. "And it's not my business if you don't wanna answer, but why?"

"I..." I'm not sure what to say, but I know Trevor will at least understand the transgender part. As for family, I've heard his mom died, so I'm not sure how he'll take my situation with her. I tell him anyway, even about last weekend.

"Wait, shit, she said you died?" he says. "That's really fucked up. It sounds like she only uses you when it's convenient for her.

"Oh, don't worry. That's not too often," I assure him sarcastically.

"Alright. Well, I am not one to judge, but it does sound like a breaking point. Honestly, I reached one this weekend too. I wanted to get the Robert thing done first, but since that's taken care of, I'm planning. We could go together, I think. I haven't told Cole yet, though, so don't mention anything to him. I want to be sure before I scare him like that. He's got a good family; I wouldn't ask him to leave. If we both go, though, he'd be alone. I just can't be here anymore, man."

"I get it. Leaving Cole seems like a dick move, but I can't live in my home anymore, either."

"Alright, well then, do you want to go together? I'm sure Randy will have a spot open for you."

"Randy?"

"Oh, Xida's dad. He runs that punk DIY club I told you about in Buschen. He's taken in LGBTQ+ homeless and the like before, so I think he'd take you in too. It's not really a homeless shelter, but it's a refuge, definitely. It acts as its own community, apparently. I'm going to try to take refuge with the punks. We could easily take the bus to the joint. Randy's expecting me this coming Friday, though, which I know may be sort of fast. I need to get out this week because of stuff with my dad. Four days is not a lot of prep time. Would you be okay with that?"

If I go to this place, I realize I could be a boy. It's a punk space. Nobody would take issue with my gender identity. I can be me. It would even help make sure the police don't find me. They're my only real concern. It's not like anyone would search for me, especially my mom. At the same time, though, I don't know these people. Trevor only knows the owner, and barely that, but I don't have other options.

"Could I be male there?"

"Of course."

I genuinely smile for the first time in what feels like forever. Finally, I can be who I am without anyone getting in my way.

"Okay then. Let's do it. I have nothing else to lose."

21

COLE

———

Rehearsals start immediately after school on Monday, so I head straight to the theater after all my classes. It makes me nervous about being there with all the upperclassmen, but Ana and Raina are there too. Raina looks irritated and continues sneaking glares at Ms. Castiel and Ms. Pasvar the entire time. She must still have the same part if she's even mad at Ms. Pasvar, since she was one of the audition judges. At the same time, the familiarity of Ana and Raina's combined energy makes me feel more comfortable. Once people realize I'm the freshman who got the part of the town mayor, they start coming up to congratulate me. I didn't realize it was such a big deal or that I was good enough for a part they all consider important. I guess Trevor was right to have me aim for the lead. I must have made a good impression.

The stage here is larger than I expected. We never had a stage this large in Plano. I can always see it from the cafetorium at lunch, of course, but it feels so much bigger being on it, facing out toward the cafeteria.

Near the end of the first rehearsal, I notice Andrew sitting out in the cafeteria, alternating between watching us and doing his homework. I can talk to him after, then. He probably wants to talk about Robert, which makes me nervous, but I'm able to block that out while rehearsing. That's the good part of playing a character. Once you're in character, you can forget the real world.

After rehearsal, Andrew stares me down from a table in the cafetorium. He wants to talk to me. He normally looks pretty serious—or maybe bored, I can't really tell—but he seems more so right now. He invites me to sit by patting the bench space next to him.

"You're a pretty good actor for someone who can't hide when something is bothering him," Andrew comments, looking at me. I feel sort of embarrassed now. "So... do you want to talk about Robert?" he asks. He seems nervous too, although he hides it well.

"Are you that worried?" I ask back. It's not that I don't want to answer. I guess I'm just still surprised, since we're not super close.

"I am," he replies without hesitation. "Everyone in this high school knows at least some people from our middle schools, and that means we have some sort of common ground coming in. You, however, are entirely new. You couldn't have known about Robert like these kids from my middle school did. You don't seem like the boldest person, either, and there are not a lot of Hispanic students here, as I'm sure you noticed."

"Yeah, I've seen a few, but Emily's the only one I really know. But I think she's half *gringo* or something."

"Do you really care if she's half?"

"Well, no..."

"Yeah, okay. Back to my earlier question. Wanna tell me anything? You don't have to. I just want to make sure you're okay and can eventually adjust to being at school here. It's rough."

"So... I do have a question, actually... How messed up is this town? Is it just the people I've been with, or does everyone have, like, a super messed up life?"

"Well, I'm not really one to talk, to be honest," Andrew admits. "However, our district is infamous for not caring about student wellbeing. From the outside, people want their kids to go here because we get good test scores, but honestly, we're all miserable. I consider myself a little more satisfied with life than other people I've seen, but my family has money. It'll just be that way. Not everyone here does. It's people like me who can dedicate everything to school, who are keeping those test scores up. People like me and those who are in distress but still manage to keep their grades up."

"How do you know all this?"

"A natural curiosity. That's how I keep my grades up. I get curious and happen to learn stuff quicker than others. School is honestly just looking at how quickly you learn and cram. I guess Robert saw me as a friend of some sort, so he never distracted me from that."

We then sit in silence. I don't want to go back to thinking about what's happened with Emily and Trevor, so I ask what homework Andrew is doing. He says it's the same math homework that I have, which is slightly embarrassing. A few minutes later, I get a text from my mom saying she's here to pick me up, so I say goodbye to Andrew.

***

I get curious about what Andrew said, so I look up more about Buschen. I know it's a decently famous city, but I don't know much about it compared to people who live here. Most of my search online is mainly recommendations for restaurants and concert venues, but I see Refew come up on one of the schedules. That's Xida's band! They seem to perform weekly at this one place, which is pretty cool. I had no idea Xida's band was popular enough for a weekly concert. Wanting to know more, I look up Kairi Kenji, Trevor's mom. I see tons of links to articles about nonprofit stuff like what Trevor mentioned—helping out during natural disasters, serving people food and water in the summer, working with special needs children, promoting other nonprofits in the area, and even providing school supplies for students and teachers in the Buschen school district. She even had a nickname: Aunt Kai. Now I can see why so many people showed up at her funeral. Trevor must have read these articles countless times before, seeing as he knows all about what his mom has done.

It makes me oddly sad at first, especially because they're so old, but then I sort of end up just staring at the screen, thinking about it. All the time she spent helping out people, Trevor admired her so much as a kid growing up even though she was gone, wondering how Buschen is without her. It seems odd that Trevor gets bullied in Rosedale when his mom was so influential. Maybe he just doesn't mention it to those who bully him. I can't blame him there. They don't know anything about Trevor. I guess I don't, either.

22

EMILY

———

"So, Trevor, this Randy guy knows I'm coming too? And it's okay with him?"

"Yeah, it's all planned, man. He's done this before. Don't worry about it."

"I can't believe I'm doing this."

"You can change your mind whenever you want. Nobody is forcing you."

"No, I'm doing this. I have to. It's the only hope I have for living."

"I relate to that..."

"Well, you know what imminent mortality feels like, right? I feel like that's worse."

"I'm not here to compare trauma. I am legitimately worried my dad might end up killing me, though."

"Wait, what?"

"Right, I never told you. I guess it's only fair, considering you told me your story. It'll help me practice for when I tell Cole, anyway."

"Ugh, I feel bad leaving Cole..."

"Yeah... like I said before, I'd never ask him to come with us, though. I plan to give him some of the things I won't bring with me. Some stuff that helped me be who I am today."

"That's not a bad idea. I should do that too. I feel bad for him after everything that's happened."

"It's not your fault."

"I'm still going to think it is."

"Fair enough. Anyway, about my situation. So, my dad got crazy drunk on my mom's death anniversary last Saturday. I went to go visit her grave with Xida and Cole, and my dad was passed out by then. When I got back home, though, he was conscious, but he seemed to think I was my mother. There was something besides alcohol at play. I tried telling him I wasn't Kairi, but he wouldn't snap out of it. He ended forcing himself on top of me..."

"You don't mean... he...?"

"I do... I tried resisting, and he pointed his gun at me. Normally it's empty when he threatens me, but a shot went off and, luckily, hit the wall behind me. I still can't believe it. Sure, he's been physically abusive before, but not like that. So, I called Xida after, and they said they'd take me in. They had always offered, but I stubbornly refused until now. I have to leave, even if it means not seeing my mother or her house, poorly maintained as it is now, for a long time."

"Holy shit, dude... I'm so sorry."

"Thanks. But yeah, our situations are not really comparable, huh? But at the end of the day, we're still just two teens with angst and issues. Two freaks."

"Maybe so. This is just so surreal."

"Reality is stranger than fiction, you know. How are your arms?"

"They're okay, I think. Just scabbed over. Trying to hide it takes effort, though."

"I bet. Anyway, when should we tell Cole? We should tell him and him only."

"Agreed. Maybe the earlier, the better. It gives him time to process and realize the last few days are, in fact, the last days. Would he stop us, though?"

"I don't think so. If he does, then I'll talk to him."

"How about PE tomorrow?"

"To talk to him? That should work."

"Okay. So, we're really doing this. Huh, Trevor?"

"Yep. Putting everything on the line. For our futures."

"Once we finally create some."

23

COLE

———

It feels so weird that it's already the middle of the week. Two days of rehearsal have gone by, and I've somehow managed to keep up with all my schoolwork. Things finally seem relatively normal. I could get used to this.

In PE, though, I get a weird feeling from Trevor and Emily, who are on the bleachers by the time I get to the gym. They both look at me seriously, like Andrew did yesterday. It sends a shiver down my spine.

After changing into my PE clothes, I head to the bleachers and greet Trevor and Emily as usual. When I ask what's up, they look at each other, shifting uncomfortably. The tension is so thick I feel myself disconnecting mentally again.

"Is it bad?" I look at both of them to see their reactions. I still can't tell. It's scaring me more.

"Cole, before I say this," Trevor starts. "I just want you to know we can't have this known to anyone. Also, if you get mad or whatever after hearing it, I get it if you just want to leave for a while. We'll understand."

"Trevor…" I almost whine.

They're starting to really scare me. How bad is this? They said it's bad for me. Does that mean it's good for them? What could that be? Why can't they just tell me?

"This is harder than I thought." Trevor sighs. "Cole?"

"Yeah?"

"There's no easy way to say this, so I'll be my usual blunt self. Emily and I are running away."

What? I feel like I've literally been taken aback, even though I haven't moved. It can't be real. Running away? Both of them? For good? I won't see them again? It's only been two weeks. But Robert's gone now. Why are they leaving regardless? They're just going to leave me here alone?

"Are you all gonna be okay?" is the only thing that comes out of my mouth. I don't want to sound selfish.

"Um," mumbles Trevor, "you see, since last Saturday I decided to run away after what happened with my dad. I just wanted to wait until Robert was out. Emily's home life's become dangerous too, so we decided to go together. We plan to either leave tomorrow night or Saturday night. We'll be safe, though. I won't give details for obvious reasons, but I know a guy. We're really sorry to do this to you, but... I just can't live like this anymore. Apparently, neither can Emily. You have a good family from what I know, Cole, and I hope they stay that way."

"Yeah," pipes in Emily. "We figured we'd tell you now so it wasn't so sudden when we were gone. To at least take some of the edge off."

Sometimes a dull knife is worse than a sharp one.

My eyes slowly open, and I look around quickly. What just happened? Why am I in the locker room? Did I fall asleep?

"Trevor?" I ask, sitting up on what I realize is a locker room bench. I'm relieved he's here, at least. He must know what's going on.

"Hey, Cole. How are you feeling?" Trevor asks.

"What happened?" I ask.

"Well, how much do you remember?"

"Well, I remember you and Emily telling me you were running away... and both of you telling me why after. Um, I assume we got here at some point... I don't remember anything else."

"Really?" he asks. "Hmm, you were definitely out of it, alright. We left and came here. You cried, but it was more like tears were just falling while you stared into space. Then you sort of fell asleep, and I didn't really want to wake you up for lunch."

"Wait, what happened with your dad? You never told me!"

"Oh, that..." Trevor sighs, looking down. "I was going to tell you tonight, but now's as good a time as any."

He seems nervous the whole time, but as I keep listening, I quickly realize why. His dad... hearing him talk about being assaulted freaks me out. Trevor's situation is so intense it feels as if it happened to me. I can't believe that's how dangerous his dad has been. This whole time, he was dealing with that...

"Um, so anyway," Trevor finishes, laughing nervously, "our lunch period just ended. You should head off to theater. Talk to Raina and Ana. They'll be your friends, won't they?"

"I guess so," I answer, rubbing my arm. "Just give me a few more minutes."

Trevor nods and stays with me. After an unknown amount of time, I get up and walk with Trevor out of the locker room.

When we get to the theater room, I wave goodbye to Trevor and enter in the middle of a lecture. Ms. Castiel says she has to count me tardy. I don't even know how late I am.

I sit with Ana and Raina, who asked what happened as soon as Ms. Castiel finishes her presentation. I can't tell them what happened, of course, so I just say I was at the nurse without elaborating much. Luckily they buy it for now.

Andrew finds me when school ends too, before rehearsal, to ask where I was at lunch. To be fair, whenever I haven't been at lunch, it's because Robert was messing with me. He has a right to be concerned. I tell him I had lunch with Trevor, which isn't fully a lie.

When rehearsal starts, I become the town mayor. I am no longer Cole, for some peaceful minutes.

***

Friday. The final day with Trevor and Emily. The first and only time Trevor will be at my house, and although I haven't been to many, it's my last anime club meeting with Emily. After the weekend, next Monday, they'll be... gone.

Once I get to school, I head upstairs to see Trevor and Emily. I look into the library door first, and they both have really serious looks. They must be discussing tonight. They've said they can't tell me their plans, so maybe I should leave them to discuss it. I stare at them for a while, but I get back to my senses and decide to go to the gym. Andrew comes up to me and asks how I'm doing.

"I'm fine," I lie, hoping he leaves it be. I don't want to talk about it yet. Oddly, the question rubs me the wrong way.

"Don't fucking lie to me."

Woah. Andrew normally doesn't curse. He must really care. So why am I getting mad?

"I can't talk about it," I tell him. I really don't want to think about it.

"Why not?" he asks, getting irritated. "I may not have known you for long, but I know you're not this distant or mopey. In the past week or so, you've gotten slowly more closed off and depressed. Based on what I know, it's not good, and I know I don't know the half of it. I'm your friend. So guess what? That means I'm fucking worried about you, okay?"

Maybe I've been a bit unfair to him. I can't tell him about Trevor and Emily's plan, though. I promise I'll tell him what's going on Monday, and he seems satisfied with that answer.

"Thanks, man. Sorry if I was a bit harsh, but I'm very loyal to my friends. The way you're acting… it's scaring me, almost. I'll do anything to help you, Cole. Really. I don't want to lose another friend."

I thank him sincerely and sulk off. I'm surprised that I'm so tense, almost angry. I'm not used to feeling like this. Is it frustration? I don't know. I hurry to first period to get it over with. I just want to see Emily and Trevor.

During PE, Trevor says he has something else in mind for us today than, as he says, "sitting like vegetables in the bleachers." He says we all need to "have some fun," which he says with a sinister face I can't help but smile at. Trevor starts to head down the bleachers, and Emily follows suit. We're ditching? I guess Trevor is a punk kid, after all… maybe this was inevitable. I ask if we'll get in trouble, and Trevor laughs playfully.

"Of course not. They don't care," Trevor explains. "Besides, what do we care? We're not coming back. Even if we got in trouble, it would have minimal consequences for you. We're only going out for the gym period anyway. It's not like we're ditching the whole school day."

So we sneak out of the gym, and the coaches don't even look our way. We waltz around the school for a bit. It's so peaceful when there aren't people in the halls—just the sound of the AC and our footsteps. Emily doesn't say much, so I ask her if she'll be at anime club. She says she will and for me not to worry about that. After making a round through the school, we head to the double doors by the gym. Trevor and Emily open the doors as if they were weightless.

"Are you sure we should be doing this?" I ask, realizing I sound like such a goody-two-shoes. Not that I'm not one as it is. I'm not exactly a rebel in any way. Trevor assures me that we're fine, so I follow them out. We cross the parking lot, and as soon as we reach the grass, Trevor lets out a long yell and runs into the middle of the football field in the distance, slowing down and dropping to the ground once he's done.

Oh, crud. Did he just pass out? How? Emily and I can't see him from here. We're both waiting for some indication of movement or sound, exchanging worried looks until Trevor quickly yells, "Come on!"

Emily moves before I do. She yells, although not as loud, and runs to where Trevor is. I look around to make sure nobody's watching, and I yell too. It feels so good! I yell again, stronger and louder, and I continue screaming as I run until I fall in the grass too. Trevor asks us wheezily how that felt. Emily and I pant "awesome" in sync. Trevor assures us he's okay but just needs to rest. I feel embarrassed about it, but I have to use my inhaler. Neither of them cares. It's like it's normal to them.

We lie in the grass for a bit, and once Trevor feels okay, he tells Emily they should show me what's in the woods. Emily agrees, so we all get up and walk into an opening near two trees with plaques in front of them, commemorating some random sponsors.

Just beyond the trees is a clearing, and I can see a bridge to the right beyond it. On the other side of the bridge is an area full of tall grass and various plants. To the left and right of the clearing are large oak trees. It's a nice oasis compared to the usual mass of buildings that crowd this town.

We walk through some premade paths in the trees, not that Trevor walks on them. He takes the straight shortcuts instead of going full turns in the path. It's really quite peaceful. Then we go to the bridge and look down into the creek. There are small minnows in the water as well as some water skiers and other bugs.

"Hey, look guys, a snake!"

Emily and I instinctively jump back, but Trevor leans over the bridge more. Emily peeks over cautiously to look with him. She agrees there is definitely a snake.

I am not going near there now. I am not a snake fan. I guess the snake's not moving much, because Trevor gets bored quickly. Emily is fine with looking at it, but she seems like the person that could stare at wildlife for hours anyway.

We end up in an area with tall plants, and there are butterflies and bees pollinating all over. I look down and can barely see my feet. There are more trees in the distance, but we don't go that far. We have to return to the school building soon after, anyway. I almost feel sad when we have to re-enter the cold, grey school that smells like body odor and bad food.

I sit with Emily and Trevor at lunch in the library. It's awkward, since it's our last lunch together, but it's worth it. We start out with empty conversation, but with Trevor in the room, that doesn't last long. We quietly discuss what's going to happen tonight. Emily and I will be at anime club until 5:30 p.m., which is when I'll see Emily for the last time, and Trevor will get ready to go during that time and come over to my house at around 5:45 or 6:00 p.m. Then Trevor will leave and meet with Emily at my neighborhood entrance at 7:30

p.m. I wish I could see them off. I try not to be upset and talk objectively. I don't want to be upset in my last moments with them. It ruins the whole point of enjoying their company.

In theater, Ms. Castiel tells us that there will be no rehearsal today. That's pretty convenient. I can still go to anime club. I'd almost forgotten that rehearsal could interfere. Ana asks me questions about rehearsal and whether I'm excited, but her cheery presence kind of rubs me the wrong way today. I just give short, polite answers and say I'll talk to her later.

At the end of school, I run to see Trevor at his usual end-of-the-day spot. Emily is there too. She and Trevor talk to make sure they know what to do tonight, and Emily goes upstairs for anime club. I know he'll be at my house, but it still feels like the last time I'll see Trevor. We hug, of course, and Trevor gives a mysterious smile. He says he has stuff for me too that he will give me tonight as parting gifts. He won't "spoil the surprise," though, but at least it gets me excited for tonight. He leaves with his signature two-finger wave, and I feel nauseous again.

I feel too sick and overwhelmed to go to anime club yet, so I sit in the bathroom stall to get away from everyone. I think back on what's happened since I've moved here. Meeting Trevor, finding out about Robert, getting to know Emily, what Robert did to me, my recurring dream, the graveyard, my audition, the rehearsal last week when I saw Emily and Robert, the time they told me they were running away, finding out Emily and Trevor's real lives, Andrew's outburst this morning, all of it. It comes flooding in, and I can't stop it. I start crying, and my head starts to hurt.

I can feel stuff coming up.

I turn around and throw up chunks in the toilet. Then I do it again. I think about what Trevor and Emily have told me over these past few weeks. Those good things. I've learned and done a lot with them in these two weeks, especially Trevor. Trevor's opened up what seems like a whole other world to me.

Once I calm down, I get out of the stall (after flushing it twice because of the barf stench) and look in the mirror by the sink as I wash out my mouth. After a few minutes, it's been long enough that it doesn't look like I've been crying, so I head up to anime club to see Emily for the last time.

By the time I get up there, she's already finished her last Japanese lesson. I sit in the back, as usual. Much to my relief, I don't get any stares. I must look pretty normal then. Emily sits with me as presentations go on, but I don't listen much. I try not to stare at her.

When the anime starts, she asks if I want to go outside. I decided I might as well. I want to talk to her for a while before she has to go.

We sling our backpacks over our shoulders and head into the empty, echoing hallway. Emily asks if I'm okay. I don't know how to reply, so I spit out all my fears about this, being perfectly honest and hoping she can give me some comfort. I need to vent it, even if Emily's not the best person to do it to. I mention my troubles with Andrew because he's the only friend I've really made besides Trevor. Emily thinks Andrew will stay my friend if I explain the situation to him next week. She says she knows how it is to lose friends for good, which kind of makes me feel bad for her.

She also says something I'd only really thought about once: it's only been three weeks. I still have plenty of time to adapt to high school. She tells me to make sure I seek out some friends, and she tells me one mistake she made was that she didn't let people help her.

Then she gives me a note to read, a book series, and a set of DVDs. The book series is one I've heard of before but haven't read so far. Emily says it's been one of her favorite series, and she also recommends I check out the author's other series if I like this one. I've never heard of the TV series on the DVD, either. Hilly Cobra's *Flying Circus*. She tells me Trevor would know about it and to ask him. Apparently, it's a classic British comedy show. I feel grateful Emily's given me all these gifts, and it's a relief they somehow all fit in my backpack.

"Should I read the note now?" I ask. She tells me I can decide, and I decide to read it later. It will keep her memory alive longer or something. It's already sinking in these gifts are the last things I'll have to remember her by, even if we didn't know each other for long. Then I remember something else I wanted to check on. I ask to see her forearms. She removes her bracelets so I can see. The scabs are still there, of course, but they seem better. I still feel bad about what happened. I feel worse that I don't even remember what happened.

"Emily, is this truly what you and Trevor want to do?" I ask. I know the answer, but I'm desperate to hear doubts from her. It's a last resort. Emily gives a surprisingly deep answer.

"Yes," she answers. "If we're caught, we get sent home, and everything may stay the same. We may be caught right away or in a few months. However, if we make it out, everything will change for us—hopefully for the better. It's a risk we're willing to take. We'll be watching out for each other since we'll be going together, so it'll be safer. We can't back out now because we're scared. Fear has kept us here for too long, and it has made us go through too much. If we stand against it, we have to commit."

I'm stunned by the eloquence of that answer.

A dull roar begins as the anime club kids start to leave the building. I guess that means we have to go soon.

"Woah," she says suddenly.

"What do you mean?" I ask.

"This is my last time," she says. "Talking to you, I mean. It's weird for me too." We continue to stare at each other in silence. There's not much else to say. After we hear kids starting to leave, Emily hugs me, and I hug back. Then she runs downstairs. She ran too soon... I stare at her as she runs, trying to see as much of her as I can. Even as she goes down the stairs and out of view, I don't dare tear my eyes away. I fall to my knees, still staring. She's gone too soon. That was too fast.

24

COLE

—

I don't remember getting off the floor of the school hallway, but now I'm back home in my bedroom, waiting for Trevor to arrive. This will be my last time seeing Trevor. Ever.

I try my best not to immediately sprint when the doorbell rings. Trevor comes in, greetings are exchanged, and my mom gives up a plate of empanadas and tells us to have fun. Trevor knows a surprising amount of Spanish, so he communicates with her just fine. He's not in his usual outfit, either. He's in a plain black denim jacket with a hood and plain holeless blue jeans. He changed before coming here, and he's made himself look discrete somehow. He has his backpack too, and it seems full. I can tell he's having trouble bearing the weight.

We climb up the stairs to my room, and Trevor asks what I want to do, immediately dropping his brick of a backpack with a thud. I'm not sure how to answer that, because there's so much I want to do before he leaves. I decide to say I want him to tell me all about the alternative world. That's the knowledge it seems that only Trevor can give me. I just got introduced to the punk lifestyle and music, so I want to know what all is out there. Trevor puts in a CD he brought and agrees.

Trevor tells me far more than I thought was possible to know about punks, goths, mods, teddy boys, skinheads and SHARPS, straightedges, grunge kids, metalheads, hippies, beatniks, emos, the Japanese visual kei and lolita cultures, Russian stilyagi, French zazous, German swingjugend, and tons of other kinds of people I've never heard of. My head is spinning to try to keep up, but every sentence is him still being here, not ready to leave yet.

"How do you know all this?" I ask. "Also, why are there so many labels when all of them seem to hate labels?"

"Well, I know a lot by doing research and getting to know people at concerts and through events. I've wondered about labels too, and more often than not, it's the media or society which makes them up. However, when it comes to being rejected by society for being different, being part of a group that society fears seems like something to spit in their faces. There's security in knowing your ideas fit in somewhere and that you're not the only one."

"I guess I can see that."

"To be honest, I don't think the world will ever be without labels," he continues. "I think labels only cause problems when they are not just out of solidarity. People take them so seriously. That's why they're so bad. They think a label defines who they are, or they fight over whether somebody *truly* fits under the label. Some people get so elitist about it and don't even realize it. It's a petty game to play. 'Goths' can also be punk or listen to ska, even pop music. It makes no difference. People should call themselves what they want. I call myself a punk, but if I decide to wear lace and listen to Britney Spears every so often, you know what that does, Cole?"

I shake my head no.

"It makes no difference. I'm still a punk, right? Because punk is about thinking for yourself and doing whatever the hell you want. So are many subcultures. They have different tendencies in music and expression, is all. It's a crazy game to discuss labels. I only think labels should be used for classification, for nonhuman stuff, and it shouldn't be unnecessarily specific. Ironically, music goes in that. However, if someone else thinks differently, so be it. I'm not gonna put an arbitrary label on them. Do you see how dumb it is to argue over them? Don't bother with labels, and they may go away. But don't be scared to be part of a group. Got it?"

"Uh... sure?" I answer, laughing nervously.

He laughs. I smile too. It's fun having him mess with me like this. We keep talking and listening to his CDs.

We look at the time: 7:10 p.m. I look back at Trevor. He has to go soon. Trevor takes a piece of paper and writes down the places he likes to go in town. He says he has other stuff for me too. I help him tilt over his backpack, and he unzips the main pocket, CDs spilling out like jewels. There are many well-used CDs with ghosts, chains, deformed crosses, collages, silly photos, lightning, demons, skulls, and graveyards on their covers. I recognize some of the albums from Trevor's recommendations. I look at all of them and back up at him.

"They're yours. I know you'll take care of them. I'm only taking one CD with me; my favorite album of my mom's. The rest belong to you now. The ones with the red sword stickers on them were my mom's. I know them by heart. I hope they'll help you as much as they've helped me. I've also got some classic books for you. Just for educational purposes. They'll help you understand other ideologies better than any public school will, and you can use them to make your own decisions too." The authors surprise me. Bakunin,

Confucius, Laozi, Plato, Voltaire, Nietzsche, Ronald Hutton, Vladimir Lenin... Karl Marx? Trevor's given me *The Communist Manifesto*.

"I'm not a communist, Trevor." It's all I can say. Otherwise, I'm overwhelmed. I feel like I did at anime club, but worse.

"No, of course not, neither am I," he says. "But just read them. Propaganda's gotten out of hand. Stalin and Mao ruined it by calling their left-wing nationalism 'communism.' I'm not a fan of big government, anyway. There's no way you can think for yourself if you don't even bother to interpret situations from the source and keep an open mind. Besides, you'll realize American democracy already has communism and socialism in it, and it's not always the bad stuff." I look at everything now. I place the manifesto back on the floor. I can feel myself tearing up. My chest is tightening. It's finally happening. Trevor's leaving for good, and here's the proof. Trevor notices me and hugs me as tight as he can, enveloping me in warmth. Warmth I'll never feel again.

"I'm gonna miss this," I whimper softly into his shoulder, placing my arms around his waist. I feel like a child. I shove out thoughts of my dream, suddenly rushing into my head.

"I will too," replies Trevor softly. "Thanks for being such a great friend and a great person. Trust me, there are more people like that than we may think. You just have to find them. You're loved, Cole. Don't ever feel bad about being yourself or that nobody loves you for it. If anyone hates you for it or tries to mess with you, make them shut the fuck up, courtesy of me." He weakly giggles, and I do too. "One more thing, Cole."

"Yeah?"

"If anything ever happens, get help. Please. Don't suffer through this alone. I'd hate to see you end up in a bad place...

Stay alive, Cole. I'm not fucking kidding on this one. Neither Emily nor I want you dead, nor does anyone else. Anyone who says they do is delusional and really doesn't have a life of their own anyway." Neither of us wants to let go.

It's 7:20 p.m. Trevor has to go now. He slowly backs off, giving me a quick kiss on the forehead before letting go. Trevor's never done that before, but I know it's a friendly kiss. I can just tell. My eyes have dried up for now. We both work on finding a place in my room for the books and CDs my mom would kill me for having. Most of it goes in the bottoms of my drawers, but the books without the titles on the spines go on my bookshelf like normal.

"Funny how when it comes down to it, there always seems to be no time for goodbye," he says solemnly. I nod, too upset to speak. He tells me he'll be okay.

Trevor puts on his backpack, and we both head downstairs to the entrance. I stay as close as I can to his side. I want to still feel the warmth. We fake smiles as my mom sends Trevor off. As he heads out, he looks back at me and gives his signature two-finger wave for the last time. Then my mom closes the door as he goes away. I can still see Trevor through the bits of decorative glass. Even in the distorted image, I still see him, wiping his face with his sleeve. He's crying.

I tear my eyes away before my mom notices, speed-walking to my room. I realize something when I get there. It's small, but it makes me want to scream in fear. This ending was not perfect. I forgot to ask about Hilly Cobra.

25

EMILY

I wish it were a little harder to figure out what I'm bringing with me to Randy's place. I know I can't bring electronic devices because they're easily trackable, so I can only bring my MP3 player since it doesn't connect to the internet. Other than that, I'm mainly bringing books and CDs.

The last day has finally come. It's my last day in Rosedale, last day at home, last day of high school, last anime meeting even. My backpack weighs on me more than usual, reminding me of the books and DVD set I brought for him as parting gifts. One is my favorite book series, *Max Soar*, about teenagers with wings who have to hide from the government and live on their own off the grid. I also bring a Hilly Cobra's *Flying Circus* DVD collection. Hopefully, it will help him laugh when things get harder for him.

I see Trevor in the morning, and he seems excited to leave. He says he already has all of things ready, and I tell him how I only have one bag and will pack when I get home.

I feel high and mighty in all my classes, knowing I won't be there anymore. I ignore all the teasing, and I feel this newfound confidence. Well, perhaps it's cockiness or insanity, but I'm okay with that for now. It's the same feeling as when you know you're going to die that night. However, this one is more exciting, since it's like I'm beating them as opposed to losing myself because of them.

When I sit with Cole and Trevor in PE, we try to have fun with him. We even go outside the school for a bit. Cole is really hesitant to go, but I don't mind heading outside. Nobody's going to care anyway, and if they did, we'll be gone soon anyway. It's a decently sunny day. There are a few small clouds, but they don't block the sun. We head out to the field first, and Trevor lets out a roar, running into the field before falling over. I look at Cole. We can't tell if he fell of his own accord or if he somehow passed out. My ears are still ringing from his yell as he calls for us to follow his lead. Aw, what the hell? It's my last day, and I have a lot of steam to let out.

I scream too, my paranoia preventing me from yelling as loud as possible, and I run to the field too. Cole eventually does the same, screaming his entire run. That was so awesome. We lie down in the grass for a while, looking up at the sky and feeling the wind. Trevor and Cole both need to get their breath back, but I don't mind lying there. It's calming. There are no cars, barely any people, and the bugs and birds are at peace.

Then Trevor suggests we show Cole the nature area behind the school. I remember the incident with Caston and the others, but I know that won't happen this time. So I agree, and we take Cole on a tour. It's a good place to get away, so I hope he can come by this place every so often. We go down the paths in the trees, but of course Trevor doesn't precisely follow them, being the punk he is. We also go to the stream, and Trevor spots a small snake in the water. It's really pretty, just one glossy color. It doesn't move too fast, either. Cole seems scared of snakes, though, so I don't encourage him to come see, as much as I want to tease him.

Cole also sits with us at lunch, which I obviously don't mind. I can tell Cole is upset, but he's trying his best to enjoy today before we leave. I really do feel bad for him. He has other friends, right? I want to ask, but if he doesn't, I don't want to bring up what is surely a sore spot. I might as well learn a lesson from him and enjoy this too.

After school, I head up to anime club after confirming my plans to meet up with Trevor at 7:30 p.m., leaving him and Cole some alone time. At least this isn't Cole's final goodbye, since Trevor will be at his house for a while. Cole's late for club, so I'm relieved when he comes up, even though I've already given the Japanese lesson. He sits in the back corner, as he did last time, and after a few presentations from other members (which were pretty cool, by the way), we start the anime. I sit with him, of course, and we know neither of us is really paying attention to the anime.

I whisper to him and ask if he wants to head out into the hallway. After some hesitation, he nods in agreement. I bring my backpack, and I tell him to bring his. We walk in a circle through the hallways and talk.

"Do you think you'll be okay?" I ask first. I really want to make sure.

"I don't know…" he trails. "I mean, you guys are my first friends here. Trevor has been one of the best friends I've ever had, even. The three of us. Especially me and him. No offense, we've shared and done so much in the past three weeks. Both of you have already changed my outlook on life. I can't imagine how I'd be in your situations, so I don't think I should intervene. I just came into the picture at a bad time. I'm scared too of what will happen after this. I have Andrew as a friend, but he's not open like Trevor is. I mean, I know he cares, but I don't know how he reacts to strong emotion. I don't want him to abandon me, either."

Damn. "Well," I reply, seeing his eyes begging for advice, "I don't exactly know your feelings, but I know how hard it is to have friends abandon you. In my experience, I normally didn't have other friends or people to go to, so I had to suffer myself, which, as you can see, hasn't done me well. You, however, are new. As you said, it's been only three weeks. You can still make new friends, and I'm sure that Andrew dude will help you through this. Anyone who cares even a little will help you with something so big. You also have your mom. This news will get to her regardless of what you do, assuming either the school or Trevor's dad tells the police to search for us. My mom probably won't so she can keep her lie with her boyfriend. Anyway, we do both hope you'll be okay eventually. So please let people help you, but also make sure you get time alone to let out your feelings. Do what you need to do. Don't let others tell you how to grieve, as they say. We're both really sorry for the pain this will cause you. Here."

I take out a note I'd written him this morning as a final goodbye. He looks at it and looks back up at me.

"Read it. Take it to heart. Hide it so nobody can find it. Even destroy it if you have to, although I personally wouldn't prefer that. Also, take these." Now I give him my parting gifts: the entire Maximus Ryde series in paperback and my Hilly Cobra's *Flying Circus* DVD set. I tell him what they are and what they mean to me. He seems a bit overwhelmed, but he thanks me and puts them in his backpack carefully. He asks if he should read the note now or later.

"It was meant for after I left, but if you want to, go ahead." He puts the note in his backpack instead of reading it now.

That may do him better. His eyes start to water. He asks to see my arms. I take off my bracelets and show him the scabs. I look at them too. I haven't picked at them much yet, but the temptation is definitely there. If I wait a few more days, then maybe I'll pick them just as they scar. I tell him not to upset himself over it. It was an incident we had to face to reach our goal. He asks one more time if this is really what we want, and I explain our logic behind what we're doing. Fancy phrasing comes out of my mouth, but I'm not 100 percent confident in what I'm saying.

"Wow... I understand," he replies once I finish. "I have one more concern, though, but don't kill me when I ask."

I nod.

"Do you and Trevor... like each other? That way?"

Well, that was off-putting. I calmly say no. He's seemingly satisfied with that. He says he just wanted to make sure.

My phone buzzes, notifying me we only have five more minutes until the end of club. Kids will be coming out soon to go home. I hate that reminder right now. I don't want to leave Cole just yet. When I give him the news, he hugs me. I flinch; it's been a while since I've been in a good embrace that wasn't out of malice. I'm not used to it. After I compose myself, I hug him back.

"Stay strong, Cole," I tell him. "I know you are strong. Heck, you're stronger than me. I'm weaker to be running away. If you get through this in any way, you are stronger than me. I wish you the best." Ugh, that sounded so cheesy. It was true, though. His eyes water again as we pull away. I want to tell him not to cry, but if my two only friends were going away forever where I couldn't contact them, I'd cry too.

"Woah," I gasp.

"What?" he asks. We can hear people coming out.

"This is my last time. Talking to you, I mean. That's weird for me too." We stare again. He doesn't say anything. I realize I have to go, and so I squeeze him one last time and leave him with my gifts. They'll be in good hands with him.

I hop into my mom's car and mentally flip off the school as we leave. Goodbye. We drive past the ugly green roof that holds in my suffering like a prison. It stands unassuming, quietly laughing as it hides what goes on inside its doors.

My mom drops me off in front of my house and then drives off. Luckily, she is gone. It makes all this easier.

While she's gone, I unpack my school backpack entirely. Then I gather three main outfits I can easily wear more than once, some food for the ride, some water, about five special books, a clock, my blanket, and my stuffed bunny. I clear my phone and leave it on my counter. I back up my most necessary laptop files onto my USB drive and format the laptop too.

I go to the bathroom to grab some toiletries, and I realize one more thing I want to do. I can finally do this. I grab the electric razor from the bottom cabinet and some nail scissors. I part my hair to the side a bit and pin the big part on my left down with some bobby pins. I place the trashcan exactly to my right. I grin at myself in the mirror like a madman. Then I turn on the razor.

I start carefully shaving down the right side of my head. Not all the way, but just enough to show a small bit of hair spiking out. Clumps of hair fall into the trashcan to my right, which feels oddly freeing. I then move the trashcan and cut the left side of my hair so it all matches up, and then I make it go halfway up my ear level at a slight angle down the front. I look up when I'm done. It's not perfect, but I like it. Extra hairs scratch at my neck, but I'm not bothered. I take the razor and a pack of batteries, because I'll have to shave every so often, of course.

I put on my plain black jacket, a plain black shirt, some blue jeans, and my black Converse. I figure that's a normal enough outfit. I also grab two sports bras and wear one the usual way and the other backward, flattening my chest. I look in my mirror again. I can't help smiling. I finally look somewhat like a dude. My new life is starting. As they say, this is the beginning of the rest of my days.

26

COLE

———

I wake up to the smell of eggs and bacon wafting into my room. The sounds of clacking pots, sizzling, and Mom's reggaeton cleanup music are familiar signs of the weekend. Yet, I'm not excited for the food, nor do I have any desire to go to the kitchen and talk to my mom.

Yesterday feels like I only dreamt it. When I tilt my head and see Trevor's CDs and my new books on the bookshelf across the room from me, I still can't help but think they'll be in school on Monday. That Trevor and I will share more amazing moments and that I'd get to know Emily more. Yet, the gifts remain.

My mom calls me down to eat, so I have no choice but to throw on a shirt and feign joy, even when my mom asked about my time with Trevor last night. Maybe it helps that it hasn't really sunken in yet.

After eating, I lock myself in my room. Time to see what all I've been left with. My first thought goes to Emily's note. I can read it now and, I guess, destroy it after if I felt so inclined.

I look toward the pile of new CDs on the floor by my stereo. I recognize some of the bands, so I play a Fismits album out loud as I read. It doesn't drown my mom's cleaning music, but it's loud enough that I can hear.

"Hey, Cole," it starts. "First off, I'm sorry. For everything. I know it must have been really weird suddenly being thrown into all this, especially things involving me. We didn't even get to know each other that well. The reason I left this for you is for you to know me a bit better and to explain what to do now. I have no idea how your old town was, but I've lived in Rosedale my whole life. I know how it is here, and it's important that you understand some things."

This note is almost structured like an article. She has sub-headings for the three different topics that read: My Gender, What to Expect at Central, and Advice. I sit on top of my bed and throw my thick blue plaid blanket over myself as I keep reading.

"So, something I really only feel comfortable telling you after leaving is about my gender. I'm done being a girl. I never truly was one, and hopefully, now I can live as I want—as a boy. I don't know if you know what being transgender is, but I'll try my best to explain. It basically means my gender isn't what I was assigned when I was born. That's who I really am. Even just writing 'I'm a boy' to you right now gives me a relief I've never known. I told Trevor earlier this week, so he knows why I have to leave too. Where I'm going, if we ever happen to run across each other again, I almost hope I'm unrecognizable to you."

So, Emily's... a guy? She—wait, he—has been hiding that this whole time? I can see why sh—HE told Trevor before me. He knows more about that gender stuff than me. Is it really that common? If people have to hide it, then maybe it is. I keep reading.

"After I came out to my mom, before high school, my mom started neglecting me. When she was actually acknowledging me, it was only because she was giving me shit. Last weekend she made me hide while she brought over a boyfriend and told him I was dead. That was the last straw for me. If she's that ashamed of me, I figured I might as well disappear. I have no idea if she'll try to find me or not, but I'd rather she didn't at this point."

Under What to Expect at Central, he lists people to watch out for (besides Robert, of course), teachers to stay away from, and even some teachers who are "safe." Ms. Rowan is on there, as is Ms. Pasvar.

The last paragraph of the letter reminds me of what she said about Andrew and making friends.

"Please don't go through this alone," the letter pleads. "I know you can't tell anyone what happened to us, but it's only the first few weeks of school. You have plenty of time now to move on, make friends, and have a normal high school life. I don't want you to end up like me: unable to ask for help from anyone and doing everything myself. I don't mind being cynical and jaded most of the time, but not being able to trust anyone isn't worth it. I really hope you're able to keep going as if this didn't happen. As much as possible, anyway. If things get too hard on your own in this new place, please get help. Don't do anything rash. Trevor loves you too, so don't you dare punk out on him. Well... I guess in Trevor's case, punking out is a good thing. At this point, I'm just writing to get words out. I hope it all makes sense. Good luck, Cole."

I lay back and reach out to press repeat on the CD player. It's my favorite Fismits song. Wow—couldn't say that two weeks ago. Emily's note is light on my chest but heavy through my body, if that makes any kind of sense. Emily was right about some things in the note, but not about it all. He was right about me not being alone. Andrew, Raina, Ana... there's real potential there. Heck, I even have my mom, which is more than Trevor or Emily could say. But Emily was wrong to ever suggest that I might not see her—him—again. And he was especially wrong to think I would ever destroy this note. It's staying with me until the day I get to see them both again. Until then, I'll do my best to make them proud.

I turn up the music and just barely hear my mom shout from the bottom of the stairs.

"Cole, what are you doing?"

"Punking out!" I yell with a grin before turning it back down and rereading the note—the second of what will most likely be a hundred more times. When I reach the end, I realize Emily didn't sign it. I guess because Emily isn't Emily anymore. Is he going to pick a new name? I wonder what it would be. I can't really make a guess. I close my eyes, trying to picture a new Emily as a man. All of us living our own lives, even if we don't see each other anymore. We'll all look at the same sky, at least, so we're still together, in a way. I suppose the possibilities are endless.

ACKNOWLEDGMENTS

First and foremost, I would like to thank everyone who has contributed in any way to the process of me writing this work. This includes anybody who encouraged me to write, read over my drafts, or even just made life easier for me from the time I was young. This includes former teachers, family, and friends. I am also grateful to the Creator Institute for giving me the opportunity to finally publish my work.

In particular, I would like to thank Benay Stein and Joanna Hatzikazakis for their dedication as editors to helping me make *Theory of Reality* the best that it can be. They took my angsty, six-years-in-the-making manuscript and turned it into the published novel I always dreamed of having. They made my journey so much better, and they stayed to help me when things got rough.

To all the amazing people who supported my preorder campaign as well (in no particular order): Carolyn and Richard Johnson (my mother and uncle!), Market Square Bookshop, Megan Zhong, Saachi Shenoy, Heather Simpson (yes, the inspiration for the Ms. Simpson in the book!), Heather Cain, Erica White, Meagan Hale, Alex Flores, J Devan Gentry, Shannon Simmons, Sarah Preston, Min Kang, Lysander

Wong, Marcus Munshi, Rynd Morgan, Katherine Rosner, Karen Okoroafor, Cooper Valentine, Chloe Woodstock, Carmen Gonser, Cordero Lopez, Blaise Willis, Brittney Espinoza, Esteban Pantoja, Brandon Zheng, Sean Olsen, Steven Lewis, Cole Lambo, Jasmine Beveridge, Nathaniel Hejduck, Daniel Holt, Alisa M Parenti, Mara Kouides, Saoirse Disney-McKeethen, Joey Kopriva, Morgan Gage, paj8989, Chase and Ty McNamee, Matthew Song Hamrick, Dominique D., Daniel Sedano, Annabelle Crowe, Fabiola Flores-Salazar, Eric Koester, Kelly Coons, Matthew Easterling, Despina Collins, Yuki Waugh, Jamie Miles, Naoko Ozaki, Shifa Rahman, Nabeeha Qazi, TNTcon80, Valerie Hellmer, Shannon Cheng, Jackie Fain, Jacob Tate, Sara Mendiola, Eden King, Mikki Hebl, Nea Daniel, Anna Margaret Clyburn, and Julia Shi.

So many of you are people I've had the honor of getting to know throughout my life, and I'm disappointed I am unable to describe individually how you all made a difference, inside and outside of my publishing journey. Just know anyone who has remained my friend, mentor, or other positive influence on my life is somebody I hold dear to me. Even if we don't talk much, I still think about you all, including those of you not listed above.

I would also like to thank the Pride and Latine communities at my university for allowing me to incorporate some of their experiences into my novel. I learned a lot from these experiences about my own LGBTQ+ and Latine identities, and I have worked hard to ensure they are represented in a relatable way.

Lastly, I would like to sarcastically thank anyone who made my life miserable. You all were the reason I started writing *Theory of Reality* all the way back in middle school. Your continued efforts and oddly insistent dedication to this cause have given me motivation and content ideas that I hope others like me will be able to relate to since you all aren't that creative.

WORKS REFERENCED

──────

NOTE FROM THE AUTHOR

Merriam-Webster. s.v. "intersectionality." Accessed March 15, 2021, http://academic.eb.com/EBchecked/topic/600338/Arturo-Toscanini.

Made in the USA
Middletown, DE
18 November 2023